The
CHRISTMAS
CONNECTION

A Jemima Fox Mystery

JOSIE GOODBODY

First Edition published in 2018 by Goodnight Books

This Second Edition published in 2019 by Goodnight Books

For my beloved son, Arthur, on his first birthday

19th December 2018

Chapter 1

Mayfair, London
16th October 1946

The Duchess of Windsor stepped out of the double doors of Cartier onto Old Bond Street. Small, slender and yet somehow imposing with her angular face and immaculately dressed figure. She was followed by the harassed person of Jean-Jacques Cartier himself, piled high with her bags. Striding across the pavement, with a few clicks of her narrow crocodile skin heels, she stepped up into a sleek black Bentley. Monsieur Cartier barely had time to arrange the bags on the seat next to her, when without so much as turning her head to acknowledge his farewell, the Duchess had ordered her departure. "Driver, to Claridge's."

Once inside the purring car, Wallis looked down at the three red embossed Cartier bags on the soft leather beside her – all sealed for safety. Opening her handbag with a snap, she pulled out an exquisite pearl-handled penknife, and slit the ribbons holding the largest bag shut. She had never had the time or patience to undo knots and the severing of the silk was so much more satisfying. Putting her gloved hand inside, she pulled out the red leather, gold embossed box that lay within and paused for a moment to savour the weight of it.

Ever since she had first mesmerised the future King of England some fifteen years earlier, Wallis Simpson had encountered jewels that most people would never have even dreamed existed. Rumours that he had spent in the region of £1 million were not far off. Diamonds as big as quails' eggs, emeralds that glittered like green fire, sapphires the colour of the purest depths of the ocean and deep red rubies set in necklaces like drops of the finest of wines – pigeon-blood red, the jewellers called them – which the Prince of Wales had lavished upon her until she nearly stooped under the weight of them. These jewels, however, were different.

She had never meant it to have gone so far. She had been quite happy before they were married when, still wedded to Ernest Simpson, she had been flattered by the attention of the besotted then Prince of Wales. The jewels he gave her had been put by, saved for a time when she would be usurped as mistress by another – after all, isn't that what kings had? Mistresses? She had been content – and aspired only that her role would perhaps continue when the prince inevitably came to the throne as Edward VIII. But no, David had wanted to marry her. Instead of his obsession with her waning and cooling, if anything it became more fervent as each year passed. And so, she had had to divorce poor Ernest, and marry a man who would no more grow up than Peter Pan. The jewels he gave her were things of beauty, and happiness and power. The coldness of the precious stones on her skin became a comfort, in a love affair she could not reciprocate.

She held the heavy leather case gently in her hands and felt a little shiver of excitement. Inside was her surprise for him, and for them; his family. Hidden in the case held in the Duchess of Windsor's hands was a diamond tiara worthy of an empress. Enormous emeralds set against hundreds of diamonds – the most powerful of stones – on a diadem topped with five heavenly stars; more a crown than any other royal tiara. The emeralds matching perfectly her emerald engagement ring; a nineteen-carat Moghul emerald, that Cartier had found him in Baghdad. The emerald that had given her the idea for this little plan. Despite herself, Wallis let out a little laugh, *if only these jewels knew what I have in store for them.* She had been advised against wearing regal headwear in London by advisors concerned how it would look – the twice-divorced American parading herself as if she were a blue-blooded princess. She hadn't even been allowed access to the Royal Family's collection of jewels, as was her right, but this tiara was different. The priceless emeralds had been left to her husband by his grandmother, Queen Alexandra who had been given them by her sister, an Empress of Russia. These stones remained David's personal property after the abdication and not the property of the Crown, despite their vast value. The Royal Family were furious that Wallis has managed to keep her hands on such important heirlooms. The creation of the tiara with these famous gemstones represented all Wallis and David yearned for – beauty, stability and their rightful place in the lineage – and, although sapphires were the Duchess's favourite, she knew emeralds were said to be a talisman to ward off evil and was glad of it. She slid the leather box back into its bag. Once David was back from speaking with his brother with the news that finally, she would officially be recognised as a member of the Royal Family and called Her Royal Highness; and that he had a role worthy of his status, she would wear it for dinner to celebrate with the Dudleys.

"We have arrived, Your Grace," the driver said through the dividing glass, and Wallis snapped back to the present moment. Checking her elegant gold watch, she saw that it was 6pm; David should be in their suite by now. She left the car, nodded at the doormen as they opened the heavy black doors and strode through the exquisite atrium, carrying her handbag and Cartier bags.

Just as the Duchess was about to ascend the staircase, she heard a familiar voice calling "Your Grace!" and Laura Dudley appeared at the other end of the hall. Her husband, the Earl of Dudley was an old friend of the Duke. Wallis and David were not allowed to stay in any of the Royal residences while in England, but the Dudleys kindly lent them their Sunningdale home, Ednam Lodge, while they themselves decamped to the hallowed suites of Claridge's. To Wallis, not being allowed to stay in the Royal residences was both abhorrent and unbearably petty, but she felt sure this would change once she was an HRH – she had waited ten years after all. And, she thought, hadn't she more than proved herself as the Bahama's First Lady during the war? Like Laura Dudley, and much of the female aristocracy, she had worked for the Red Cross as a nurse during the war.

"Wallis, David's not back yet. William has sent a message to Jane and the Fairfaxes to delay dinner until 9pm."

"Oh actually the young Fairfaxes are coming for tea tomorrow instead."

"Very well, in the meantime, could I invite you up to our suite for tea now?"

"Tea?" said Wallis looking at her gold Cartier watch. "I'd rather a cocktail, Laura dear. After all it's just past six o'clock. Shall we sit in the bar? I don't want everyone to think that I'm still hiding away."

"Well…" Laura shuffled. "I don't know if William would like that. He's quite of the stance that we shouldn't be seen drinking cocktails in public."

Wallis had to keep from rolling her eyes. "Oh Laura dear, since the war anything goes. Come on, it's not like we're going to be sitting in a public house."

Secretly, Wallis really wanted to sit at the bar to show off her new purchases, even if it was just the bags. No one knew what was inside, which was part of the mystique behind her, but she knew the crimson bags emblazoned with Cartier would evoke such lust and jealousy in her fellow guests' eyes. After years of listening to the rumours that had been created and spread about her since her and David's relationship became common knowledge, Wallis was quite happy to inspire a little envy. And to hell with drinking in public, she'd been married to David for over a decade and had nothing to hide. As Duchess of Windsor, she had done her duty being first lady of the Bahamian backwater and now she was back in London, about to be acknowledged by the Royal Family for the first time. She didn't care who saw her taking a cocktail with bags of jewels in one of the city's finest hotels – and after all, half of Europe's exiled kings had spent the war holed up in Claridge's.

The two exquisitely dressed ladies, one far more bejewelled than the other, made their way into Claridge's cocktail bar and took a discreet corner table, Laura nipping a furtive glance over her shoulder. Wallis arranged her bags next to her on the dark blue velvet banquette and pulled out a gold cigarette case.

"Laura, order two glasses of champagne cocktails will you please," she requested as she lit a slim cigarette, already positioned in an ebony holder.

The champagne arrived, and the two ladies took a sip each before resuming their talking.

"Do tell me what you have collected from Cartier, Your Grace," Laura asked, knowing Wallis was waiting for her to enquire. Laura, twenty years younger than Wallis and not nearly so assured, also knew that the Windsors expected even close friends to address Wallis as 'Your

Grace' to make up for not being titled Her Royal Highness.

"Oh, these?" Wallis gave a little laugh. "Well, David – so adorable – ordered me some trinkets that I had to collect, isn't that sweet of him? And then I had something rather exciting to pick up too; those emeralds he gave me – do you remember?"

They were interrupted by the manager of the hotel rushing nervously over to their table.

"Your Grace, Your Ladyship." He bowed. "I am afraid that there has been some terrible news from Ednam Lodge."

The Countess of Dudley, who was missing her lovely home and loyal staff, despite spending the week in the most beautiful of Claridge's suites, gave a small squeak.

"What is it – what has happened?" Laura felt sick. She had never wanted to lend the Lodge to the royal exiles, but her husband was an old friend of His Royal Highness's and was strongly of the opinion that it was a bit much, King George not letting them stay in any of the royal palaces or apartments.

"It appears that there has been a burglary. The Earl is on his way to you now," said the manager, just as in strode the Earl of Dudley, tailed by a very down-beaten Duke of Windsor.

"Terrible news, what!" boomed the Earl.

The Duke winced. "My dears, I really think we should go somewhere private," he murmured.

"But our champagne has just arrived!" Wallis

protested.

The two men looked at each other. David spoke first, "I'm afraid you might need something a little stronger."

Chapter 2

Sunningdale, Surrey
16th October 1946

He'd just been instructed to take the emeralds – big, loose green stones, impossible to miss, was what he'd been told. Anything else he managed to steal was his to keep, or indeed sell. It hadn't been a hard decision to take the job; both his wife's and the twins' birthdays weren't far off, and he had barely nothing for his family – he'd not been able to work properly since the end of the war. He was a local lad, he knew some of the gardeners up at the big house from the pub, knew the lay of the land and his wife was friends with a couple of Lady Dudley's maids – everyone knew everyone in these parts. Like most of the villagers he was also incensed that the kind Earl and Countess had been turfed out of their home by the ex-King and his fancy American wife. Approached in the pub one evening by a nondescript man in a tidy dark suit, it wasn't a difficult decision to liberate a few of the trinket-laden Duchess's jewels and make a few extra bob on the side. After all, he reassured himself, with the amount she had it wasn't like she would miss them.

At five-thirty, when he knew the house staff were downstairs in the basement taking their tea, he took a ladder to the fourth window in from the East Wing as he'd been instructed. The room had a chilling feel to it – as the Duchess was away no fire had been lit, and with most of her belongings packed away the room looked bare. He let himself down from the window ledge to the wood planked floor as quietly as possible and looked around for the leather case he'd been told contained the Duchess's jewels. He spotted it tucked away, looking almost forgotten by the fireplace. It was heavy, reinforced with metal bands and three locks, and much bigger than he'd expected. He didn't dare open it to check that the emeralds were inside – there wasn't time to pick the locks, and if he got caught he risked a lifetime in prison. Could this even be called treason? There was no way of hiding it on himself – the box was as big and heavy as his wife's suitcase. He started to panic, should he try and open it and take the green stones from inside? No, it would take too long, he had to take the whole thing with him. It was much too heavy to carry one handed while climbing a ladder, so he undid his belt and slid it through the handle of the box, strapping it around his body like a large and bulky messenger bag. He climbed back on to the sill and put one leg out, feeling for the top rung of the ladder outside. Just as he was swinging the other one over, he heard a creaking coming from outside the door of the bedroom. A sudden surge of adrenaline overtook him and as he saw the door handle turn he was out of the window – with no time to step down each of the twenty or so rungs, he put his boots either side of the ladder and slid down all the way, catching a few splinters in the palms of his hands. He hadn't managed to shut the window, but above he could hear someone complaining. "Beryl's left the window open again – honestly, that girl is so absent-minded!"

He'd got away with it so far. Lying the ladder along the flower bed below, he ran along the outskirts of the house to where he knew the gardeners' building was, the box bumping uncomfortably against his hip, and waited in the safety of the shed, catching his breath and watching the sun set on the façade of the house.

By just after six o'clock it was dark enough to make his next move. Carefully checking that no one was around, he was sure someone would have discovered the box was missing by now, he crept slowly through the copse of birch trees – fast movement would attract more attention from any sharp-eyed ground staff who might be on the lookout. The case, still strapped to his back, was beginning to hurt, the very heavy fastenings digging in. As he left the copse of trees he took a false step and the weight and cumbersomeness of the box caused him to drop to his knees. He had thought he was in a field but now realised it was a golf course he knelt on; the grass was as pristine as that he had ever seen. It should be almost pitch black now, but the moon was up and bright, and with no uproar coming from the house he decided his best choice was to open the case and take just the emeralds – after all that was what had been instructed.

With the piece of wire that he always had in his coat pocket, he fiddled with the lock and after not long at all it clicked open. He slowly opened the lid, suddenly unsure of what he was going to find. The moonlight hit the contents of the box and he almost fainted. He knew nothing of jewellery except what he occasionally saw in the magazines his wife's boss gave her of glamorous film stars and the Royal Family. He knew the Duchess of Windsor was hated by the Royals and had also heard rumours that she had helped the Nazis – that was one of the reasons he'd wanted to take the job in the first place. But he'd never realised how rich the Windsors must be. Glinting in the box was a sparkling stone for every colour of the rainbow, and huge at that – the size of bantams' eggs. Bracelets with white stones and pale blue stones, earrings with yellow stones and dark blue stones, and then a beautiful bird made up of more white stones, brooches, rings, a huge red stone on a ring, and then loose gems in every colour littering the bottom of the box – all except green. Once he had got over the shock, he meticulously lifted every section, opened all the little drawers, but there were no green stones, except a few smaller ones already set in pieces of jewellery. There was a string of pearls, large creamy white pearls, which as he pulled out he remembered his wife hated. She thought they were bad luck, saying that they had been inside oysters and ever since she was sick from an oyster he had bought for her in a public house for her birthday she didn't trust them. A noise behind him made him turn, but he couldn't see anything in the darkness. A fox? Either way, he didn't have time.

Shoving his pockets full of what he could manage, he left the remaining jewels on the grass and stumbled back to the farm track in the gloom. He had left his bicycle somewhere in a hedge along the lane – he'd retrieve it in the morning. As he hurried down the dark tracks back to his cottage, he wondered how on earth he was ever going to explain that there were no emeralds to the man in the neat suit.

On the dew drenched turf of the dark golf course, the string of pearls lay, glowing in the moonlight.

Chapter 3

Claridge's Hotel, London

The Duchess stormed into her suite slamming the door in the Duke's face. As she threw the Cartier bags on to her bed, she could hear him knocking.

"Please let me in. I tried my best, but they were having none of it. Cookie was standing behind Bertie throughout the whole thing, she barely let him get a word in edgeways. Now please let me in. We need to discuss the theft."

My God he is so pathetic, thought Wallis as she stalked around her room. In her temper over her husband's inability to bargain with his brother, and his wife, the news of the robbery had barely even registered, but now the revelation started to seep through her consciousness. She had never wanted it to come to this. All she had got out of it was a made-up title anyway. Except the jewels – she always knew that she had the jewels, but now so many of them had been stolen. Who would even have known where she kept them when travelling anyway?

So few people had access to her belongings. The possibility that it might have been an inside job flitted across her mind and in the same moment she was suddenly certain. It had to have been David's family trying to get his grandmother's emeralds back, those bastards! she thought. Unluckily for them, the emeralds were already set in the most extravagant of tiaras, sitting in a bag on her bed. And she smiled.

They hadn't given her the HRH she'd wanted, and she had no intention of returning the emeralds to the Royal Family. What's more she could see a way to profit from the loss of her other jewels. A plan started to weave in Wallis's mind, but she would need David to orchestrate it. And she would have to dispose of the tiara for the time being, if her plan was to work. After all she couldn't be seen with it until this had all calmed down. But where could she put it? She did have a few tricks up her sleeve. Although she had been enjoying flashing her Cartier bags about in the Claridge's bar earlier, it had not been Cartier who had made the tiara. The delightful Jean-Jacques Cartier had merely been helping his famous client by conveying her new piece of jewellery from a Parisian colleague to his Old Bond Street store, where Wallis could pick up the tiara securely. Cartier themselves had no idea of the original size or potential provenance of the emeralds, and would have not known that they had briefly held in their hands some of the most expensive jewels in the world. They were used to the best gemstones, after all look at her engagement ring. What's more, the colleague,

Jacob Levy, was far too in awe of her to ever spill the beans about the enormous emeralds he'd recently cut into brilliants and pear shapes from the uncut stones she'd presented him with. Not only would Wallis be able to say the immensely valuable emeralds had been stolen in the heist, but Lloyd's of London would pay out the insurance, David's family would never be able to claim the emeralds were still in Wallis's possession without incriminating themselves. Once the furore had died down, the Duchess of Windsor would be able to don her crowning tiara, bedecked with the emeralds her husband had rightly inherited from the Empress of Russia, through his grandmother.

She walked towards the suite's door and opened it. David was leaning against the opposite wall smoking a cigarette with a sorrowful look upon his face. Wallis was strongly reminded, and not for the first time, of the irony that while she had never wanted children, she was now married to one.

"Come in then! We can't have the whole hotel hear their rightful King sounding like a baby." She admonished him cruelly. "First we need to work out what to do about the jewels. Did they take any of the Fabergé eggs you had there?"

"No. They didn't," the poor man said guiltily. "They only took your case, none of mine."

The injustice swelled in Wallis's breast. "Your damn family! This never would have happened if they'd let us stay at Fort Belvedere, our old home, or any other appropriate Royal residences. And then they won't officially honour me with what is rightfully mine – as your wife I should be a Royal Highness, and everyone knows it!" David was shaking against the wall against the force of his wife's temper and was beginning to look oddly flushed.

"However," Wallis continued, "I am certain it was your family. Looking to steal your grandmother's emeralds that you gave me, I'm sure of it. Sarah Fairfax asked me about them in Paris and I have no idea how she would have known you gave them to me, unless someone in your family told her. Cookie no doubt." And again, she thought how clever she'd been to come up with that name for the current Queen of England, who had apparently been born to the French cook impregnated by her father the Earl of Strathmore.

"Well we might as well make the best of this dreadful situation," Wallis continued. "You must get the man from Lloyd's to come here tomorrow, or meet us at the Lodge, and we can get the insurance money for the lot."

"Yes, I suppose that you are right." David lit another cigarette with a shaking hand.

"And, if it wasn't your family then it must have been the Dudleys' staff. Who else knew that we weren't there tonight?" Wallis probed, irritated by her husband's lack of reaction.

The Duke didn't answer, he was still shaken by the whole evening but more so with the afternoon he had with his brother at Buckingham Palace. Not only had he failed to establish recognition for his wife as an HRH, Bertie had refused to give him any other official role after the Bahamas, and still he was not allowed to live back in his beloved England.

The Duchess, however, was seething over with plans. She'd remembered meeting an heiress in Palm Beach five years earlier, whose father had made his money in a chain of shops. When they had been exiled to the Bahamas. Jessie Donahue (whom she'd had to reluctantly admit had a jewel collection to rival her own) had once experienced a jewel heist. It had been one of the great mysteries of the era in New York City at the time, and even when Wallis and she met it was still a great scandal. It had been several decades before she had admitted that it was her husband who had stolen the jewels, and she had only found out after his suicide. Jessie had only admitted this to the Duchess in greatest confidence, and now Wallis felt it was time for her to return the favour. The Donahue family would keep Queen Alexandra's emeralds, set in the tiara, with their collection, safe and secret, while Wallis claimed they had been stolen. The Royal Family, Wallis had decided, deserved to be punished.

"Call him now, David."

"It's 7pm!"

"And YOU were the King of England!"

Chapter 4

The Sunningdale to Dorchester Train
19th October 1946

Three days later, on a train speeding towards the West Country, the thief finally let himself relax. The day after the theft, he had surprised his wife, currently fussing over their two boys on the seat next to him, by suggesting that they take a little holiday to visit his cousin Eric in Dorset – the first holiday they'd had together since before the war. His wife had been too wrapped up in the boys to question further the sudden departure; she had dutifully packed their cases, boarded the train and was now wiping sticky patches of jam off the children's faces, while telling them how nice it would be to see where Daddy had been on holidays when he was little. The thief settled into the seat of the third-class carriage and stole a furtive look out of the window.

He hadn't told his wife about the jewels. If he was found out and she was questioned, or God forbid the house searched, he didn't want her to be under pressure to lie to the police, or indeed explain why she was hoarding thousands of pounds worth of jewellery. He'd been terrified of telling the man in the tidy dark suit that there were no emeralds – what if he didn't believe him? But oddly the man had accepted his story without question – it was almost as if he'd know there was a chance the jewels wouldn't be there. The thief had offered the man in the dark suit the rest of the jewellery he'd taken but been waved away – told to keep it for himself and paid handsomely in used notes. It was all very strange.

He was glad to be going to Dorset, back to the cottage on the Fairfax Estate he'd visited every holiday as a boy. He'd spent an idyllic childhood running loose around the park with his cousin, like all the estate workers' children had done. Summers were spent scrounging fruit in the orchards, camping out with the local scouts and cooking delicious sausages sent down by the tiny, doting Lady Fairfax and paddling in the sea along the estate's private beach. In winter, he'd helped on the farms, mucking out and haying the animals, and sneaking into the warm pub at the end of the day to sit by the fire at his father's feet and listen to the locals' stories. And, of course, he'd been exploring. He and Eric knew every inch of Fairfax Park. They knew about the secret tunnels from the cellars to the icehouse, how to sneak through the roof space of the stables, which hollow oaks in the park you could hide your stash of sweets in and, best of all, the depths of the darkest crypts by the church – crypts so deep he wasn't even sure if the current incumbents of Fairfax Park were aware of their extent. It was in these crypts, behind a loose stone of a monument to a Fairfax relative who'd died sometime in 1729, that he intended to hide the jewels.

It was the best plan, he had decided. There was no way he could move on such a vast hoard of jewels without it looking suspicious. The payment from the man in the dark suit had been very generous, so he didn't immediately need the money, and he'd decided it was better for all if, should the jewels be discovered, they were miles away from him and his wife with no risk of incrimination. Added to this, the crypts at Fairfax Park were unlikely to be disturbed, and visiting his cousin gave him just the excuse he needed to drop in and pick up a few jewels at a time to sell on, over the coming months and years. It seemed ideal. As for the jewels themselves, they were currently hidden in his socks and underpants in the suitcase he shared with the boys. He just needed to retrieve them and put them in the old red canvas bag he had, before his wife unpacked. But, although he kept a close eye on the case, the further he got away from Sunningdale railway station and Ednam Lodge, the happier he was.

They pulled into Salisbury station, halfway along the journey to Dorchester, and he turned to look out of the window. He was just wondering if it was time to ask his wife to unwrap the sandwiches for lunch when movement on the platform caught his eye – a mail boy waving a newspaper and wearing a sandwich board across his body which was emblazoned with the headline:

DUCHESS'S DIAMONDS DISAPPEAR!

Without saying a word, he got up from his seat, opened the door of their compartment and, ignoring his wife's cries, he ran down the carriage before jumping on to the platform. Just as he handed over the coins for a copy of the paper he heard the guard's whistle blow again and turned back to see his wife and sons' faces at the window looking astounded. Running back, jumping up on to the train he managed to get through the door just as the porter was about to close it.

"You were lucky, mate!"

He walked breathlessly up the carriage, his heart thumping, to his compartment and saw his family staring at him in amazement.

"I wanted the paper," he explained and tried to shrug nonchalantly before sitting down and looking at the front page.

There was a picture of the Duke and Duchess taken outside the front of Ednam Lodge, a short piece on the scandal of the robbery, and a list of the jewellery which had been taken – much of which was sitting in his case above his head. The thief squirmed uncomfortably. At the bottom of the list were the words "et cetera" and then another short piece, which explained that added to this list were a set of incredibly valuable emeralds, possibly worth more than the rest of the jewellery put together, which had once belonged to Queen Alexandra, the King's grandmother – who'd been given them herself by her sister, the penultimate Tsarina of Russia. The paper went on to say that Lloyd's of London had paid them £25,000 in insurance money. Twenty-five thousand pounds, thought the thief. The suitcase he had left on the seat next to him was now drawing his eye as if it was magnetised. He'd known the jewels were valuable, but hadn't realised quite how much they were worth. Leaning back, he let the paper drop to his lap where it slid down to the floor. It was now imperative he moved the jewels to the crypt at Fairfax Park before they were found. Worth that amount, he was risking more than prison if they were found to be in his possession – he was risking his family's lives.

Chapter 5

Mayfair, London
23rd December 2010

It was the afternoon before Christmas Eve and Bond Street was buzzing. People trailed boxes and bags of all shapes and sizes, emblazoned with the names of all and every designer store on the street – from Dior to Dolce & Gabbana, Gucci to Graff – under the sparkling Christmas lights. The street appeared as though it were paved with gold.

Jemima Fox-Pearl and Flora Fairfax stood in Garrard, the historic jewellers to the affluent and aristocratic, waiting to collect Viscountess Fairfax's newly polished tiara for her to wear on Christmas Eve. When Flora's mother, a wealthy American heiress, had married into the family and eventually assumed the title, she had insisted on changing the traditional celebratory Christmas Day lunch to a sumptuous white tie affair on Christmas Eve – claiming it was what the Royal Family did. She also insisted that the women present wear 'family jewels', and should any female guest be unlucky enough not to be in possession of her own, Lady Fairfax would lead them to the family safe and withdraw some of the Fairfax's enormous collection. Many a delicious dinner had been passed in ridged upright posture by the unlucky guest who'd been lent a tiara much too big for her – and who had to keep her chin stiffly raised to avoid priceless antique diamonds falling into the soup. Jemima was looking forward to the opportunity to dress up, particularly in the Fairfax's sumptuous assortment of jewels. Jemima and Flora had been friends since they were ten years old and shared a dormitory at their little Dorset prep school, but it would be Jemima's first Christmas at Fairfax Park.

The House of Garrard had, over the years, created some of the most beautiful jewels that adorned the Queen and her family – including the Princess of Wales's sapphire and diamond engagement ring. However, despite her fascination with their incredible pieces, Jemima was feeling restless and tired. She'd been holed up in a Claridge's suite last night with the handsome Danny Vogel, grandson of her boss and founder of Vogel Diamonds, who for the past few weeks had proved to be utterly astounding in bed. As a result, Jemima hadn't had much sleep and was starting to feel distinctly debilitated. Danny had, however, handed over an early Christmas present as he kissed her goodbye. Beneath her blonde hair, pulled back messily into a ponytail, was a beautiful pair of diamond earrings, small flowers hanging off intricate French loops. She hadn't told

Flora about Danny yet – Flora, who liked to play it safe, would have been scandalised and accuse her of playing with fire. Jemima was also feeling guilty that she'd left the office early that day after wishing her girls in the Press Office a Merry Christmas, claiming she had to rush to get a train to Dorset. They hadn't particularly, seemed to mind – someone had snuck in a bottle of Bollinger and with no releases to write or photographs to sift through, the girls were getting drunk and reading *Tatler* articles to each other – however, as Head of Department, Jemima felt it was a bit cheeky to leave early.

"I wonder how long this is going to take?" she said out loud, shifting from one foot to the other. Under an ancient mink coat of her grandmother's, she was wearing the dress she'd been to dinner in the night before and her gorgeous stilettos were starting to pinch.

"Jem, you love jewellery stores! What's with the rush?" Flora laughed, "And why do you keep looking shifty? Have you pinched something!" Flora, still her Stella McCartney work uniform of a black cashmere jumper and Stella jeans, looked her up and down, mock-suspiciously. "You're still in last night's clothes! And those earrings look pretty new, I'm sure I've not seen them before. Christmas bonus?"

You could say that, thought Jemima to herself with a giggle. "Of course not, darling, don't be silly! You know the Vogels are really funny about their staff being in other jewellery stores – I just don't want to be caught, especially as I shouldn't really have nipped off early."

"Calm down," said Flora, "Look, the man is on his

way back with Mummy's tiara and then we can head up to Claridge's to meet Henry. I'm sure he's propping up the Fumoir Bar with yet more of his gorgeous but unsuitable friends." Flora winked at Jemima. Her brother's terrible taste in cronies had got him into trouble more than once.

"I thought we were getting the train?" said Jemima. She had woken up in Claridge's that morning – she wasn't expecting to be back so soon.

"Mummy doesn't want us carrying this on the train," Flora explained as she took a large bag from the member of staff who had just appeared. "Thank you. Right, let's go!"

"Don't you want to check it?" Jemima said, while looking absentmindedly into a display case of beautifully designed rings, huge rocks of rubies and emeralds surrounded by diamonds.

"I'm sure it'll be fine, I don't know what I'm meant to be looking at anyway!" Flora smiled at the member of staff who'd handed her the box and turned to Jemima. "There are five Fairfax tiaras and I've got no idea which this one is. I can't tell them apart anyway – you know I've got no interest in jewellery. Come on – let's go and have some cocktails."

They walked down the street, Flora holding the large Garrard bag between them, stopping occasionally to point out the lights. Jemima, towering over her smaller friend, had the oddest feeling someone was following them – underneath the noise of the shoppers she could hear the tap of metal heel tips which seemed to be pausing every time she and Flora did, but in the packed street she couldn't make out whose they were. She told herself she was just being silly – one too many gin cocktails last night must have made her a little paranoid.

"Oh, for goodness' sake," said Flora, opening her phone. "Bloody Henry's running late. He's waiting for a friend who hasn't shown up."

"A friend? Anyone we know?"

"No, someone he met over the summer I think – he's bringing him for Christmas, Mummy's furious, you know she loathes strangers around Christmas." Flora put her phone away. "I wonder what he's like? Potential Christmas fling for you, darling?"

"I'm saving myself for South Africa!" Jemima replied, relieved to be leaving Bond Street and the out-of-bound boutiques. "Flying out on Boxing Day – I can't wait. Vogel has asked me to take something out with me – I forgot to ask, is it alright to pop it in the safe when we get to yours?"

"Oh, of course," said Flora, slowing down to gaze into a window display which mostly seemed to be tinsel and one lonely bottle of bubble bath. "But no one will steal anything!"

"Talking of South Africa, thank God your brother picked up our bags yesterday – why I take so much with me, I have no idea," the further they walked the more Jemima couldn't wait to be out of last night's dress and shoes and into something clean. "Oh Flora, can we get a taxi? My feet are killing me."

"Do we have to? I wanted to walk up Bond Street and

see all the lights!"

"Yes," said Jemima firmly as she stuck out a hand. As they waited on the pavement for the taxi, she was dimly aware that a man had stopped just behind them. She presumed he wanted to cross the road, and she moved aside to let him, but he didn't step forward. She turned to see what he wanted but, just as she looked up at his face, he whirled around and strode off in the other direction.

"Flora," she said, staring after the man, "Do you recognise…"

"I'd kill for a martini," interrupted Flora as the taxi pulled up. "To Claridge's please!"

Going around the back of Bond Street and through Berkeley Square, they arrived outside the exclusive five-star hotel in a matter of minutes. Jemima paid the taxi driver, wished him happy Christmas and the girls swept past the friendly, black suited and top hatted doormen into the sumptuous atrium of Claridge's Hotel. Whenever she entered the hotel and put her feet on the chic black and white tiled floor of the large atrium, Jemima remembered what Spencer Tracy said when he died. "I don't want to go to heaven, I want to go to Claridge's." She laughed to herself – she had had a lot of visiting heaven with Danny Vogel in several of the hotel's suites. As well as in many of the other luxury London hotels after their first encounter at the Dorchester, which, coming from Dorset, she felt was just a bit too close to home.

"Why are you laughing?" Flora asked as they made their way past the huge Christmas tree in the lobby.

"Oh nothing – just happy to be leaving London for Dorset!"

"Yes, I can't wait either – and so pleased you're with us this year. Such a relief as I won't have to talk to this friend of Henry's or cousin Rupert too much!"

An hour later and the girls were happily ensconced on the sumptuous sofas of The Fumoir Bar. Jemima had been a little upset when her parents had decided to ditch the cold English weather for Christmas in sunnier climes, but after a couple of passionfruit martinis and with the prospect of a glamorous Christmas at Fairfax Park, she was feeling exceptionally cheery.

"These are delicious," smiled Flora, whose second martini was hitting her rather hard – she'd pulled off her coat and left the Garrard's box containing the tiara carelessly on the velvet seat beside her. Jemima eyed it nervously. Years of working with valuable jewellery made her intensely uncomfortable about leaving something so precious out in the open. She wished Flora would discard the eye-catching branded box.

"So, what is work making you take to Cape Town?" Flora asked leaning back. "Must be valuable for them to get Jemima Fox the Jewel Mule to go," she teased.

Jemima assumed an expression of mock outrage. "How very dare you!" She patted her bag. "Just something for a client." She leant closer. "Actually, it's the most gorgeous yellow diamond ring, but I'll show you when we're in Dorset."

"Not tempted to wear any of it for Mummy's dinner?"

Jemima made a non-committal noise and gave Flora a naughty smile. "Well, I've no Vogel tiaras with me!"

"Oh, don't worry, I'm sure Mummy will lend you something. She loves it when we're all dressed up like the Romanovs – I dread to think what relic she has in store for me tomorrow night! You're lucky you like jewellery – I was born to the wrong mother, it really doesn't interest me." She jumped up. "Can you keep an eye on the tiara while I pop to the loo?" she asked her friend, rather too loudly.

"Of course." Jemima looked down at the box which lay on the seat of the velvet chair. Curiosity overcame her and she pulled the box towards her, snapped open the clasps and peeked at what was inside. Her mouth fell open. Even in the darkness of the bar, the tiara was one of the most beautiful pieces she had ever seen. Quickly snapping it closed again, she made to pull Flora's fur coat, discarded on the neighbouring chair, over the box and stopped. Inside the bag she noticed a large envelope in thick cream paper with VALUATION printed across it. How odd, she thought, Viscountess Fairfax couldn't be selling her jewellery – she had more money than the Queen.

Chapter 6

Fairfax Park, Dorset

Four hours later, the enormous gates of Fairfax Park swung open to let in Henry Fairfax's Porsche Cayenne, full of people, presents and Jemima's huge suitcase.

"Thank God we're home," Flora murmured from where she'd been slumped across the back seat. "That was a very long drive." She exchanged a look with Jemima.

Henry's friend, John, had turned out to be a short, stocky man with a regulation military haircut and a badly-fitting slim suit. He'd greeted Jemima and Flora charmingly enough at first – but after enduring three and a half hours of being talked over, interrupted, and having to nod politely along as he described in detail every deal that he'd done that year at the bank and how big his bonus was, Flora and Jemima were quite ready to leave the car. Even Henry was beginning to look rather uncomfortable under the onslaught, and Jemima noticed that Henry's little terrier growled at John whenever he came close and had spent the whole car journey curled up on Flora's lap on the back seat, ears twitching. She couldn't help but be surprised at Henry's choice in friends. They seemed so different. Lady Fairfax would definitely describe him as NQOC – Not Quite Our Class and she tried not to giggle at the Viscountess' expression when she met her Christmas guest.

"Hen, mate, this is some gaffe!" As they drove up the twisting three-mile drive, John broke off from his latest tirade to gaze across the parkland at Fairfax Hall. Although it was dark, the gorgeous early eighteenth-century mansion was lit up like a beacon by floodlights – installed to great protestation from the rest of the family by Jessica. As they got closer the glassy lake reflected both the moon above and the huge Christmas tree, which stood underneath the central tetra-style four columned Ionic portico. Jemima stared – the beauty of Fairfax Hall never failed to amaze her, no matter how often she'd seen it. The neoclassical building, with original earlier parts, was built in the late eighteenth century by the architect Henry Holland, while the gardens were created by Capability Brown. It sat in 200 acres of Dorset parkland, not forgetting the 3000 of farmland, which swept down to the Jurassic Coast and comprised of the village Fairfield.

"Fuck, it's massive," said John. "How much is this all worth?"

Flora and Jemima gave each other a look. Is he for real?! mouthed Flora.

Hideous, mouthed back Jemima. She did, however, have the oddest feeling she'd seen John somewhere before.

"Ma and Pa are out so Mrs Wright has left us supper in the kitchen," Henry said, as they bumped through an archway strewn with ivy to a cobbled courtyard and pulled up. Lights flickered on and three large dogs came bounding out.

"Brilliant. Let's go and get something to eat, I'm starving," said Flora. "We can get the bags out later."

"I'll just grab my handbag and the Garrard bag, Flossie." Jemima called as she leant down to Flora's footwell, grabbed the very heavy bag and heaving it over she jumped out of the Porsche 4x4 with her own handbag slung over her shoulder.

She caught up with her friend who was greeting the two Labradors and a Ridgeback with hugs and kisses, they shoo'd them aside and stepped into the boot room. Jemima couldn't help but notice that John wasn't particularly keen on having a large Rhodesian Ridgeback sniffing the cashmere Ralph Lauren overcoat he'd made such a fuss over in the car and had kicked the dog away when he thought no one was looking. She really did not like this man.

Inside the huge, warm flagstone floored kitchen a large macaroni cheese lavished in cheese and glossy glazed ham lay on the scrubbed oak table.

"Who'd like a drink?" Henry asked, opening up the enormous fridge.

"Thanks, Henry, I'd love a glass of wine," said Jemima.

She quite wanted to put the ring she was carrying for Vogel into the safe before she started on the wine and, as Flora still seemed worse for wear after the cocktails, also quite wanted to make sure that Flora put the tiara somewhere safe. Not that anything would be stolen here, she reassured herself.

"Am I in my usual room? I might pop up and put a few things away." And have five minutes peace away from that wittering idiot and his sickening aftershave, she thought to herself, as John started quizzing Flora about the house and how far away it was from the family chapel. He definitely didn't strike her as the religious type! Jemima kept hold of the Garrard bag, wondering if perhaps Flora should be a little bit more careful with what she had collected for mother. She left the kitchen and made her way through the numerous rooms and corridors, before finding herself in the exquisite hall of Fairfax Hall, which was the original part of the house and dated back to the Elizabethan era. A Christmas tree which reached up to the three-storey high ceiling was impeccably decorated and there was a mountain of huge logs ablaze in the ginormous fireplace. Jemima suddenly wondered with a pang if she really wanted to be whizzing off to the Southern Hemisphere in forty-eight hours. It was so deliciously decadent here.

She climbed the sweeping imperial staircase and took the left stairs where it divided at the small landing, she hoped her room was as far away from John as possible. She couldn't help but feel that she had seen him somewhere before. The cashmere coat was like any other on Bond Street but as he'd left the car she'd seen an unusual – and particularly hideous – fur hat in his hand and could have sworn she'd spotted it somewhere else.

She made her way down a long corridor with several doors off to each side and wondered who else was staying. Lady Fairfax didn't usually like non-family guests for Christmas but did feel it was her duty to invite her widowed sister-in-law and nephew. Lady Fairfax's late brother-in-law, Richard, had been the original son and heir of the Fairfax Estate. The two brothers couldn't have been more different, characteristics particularly emphasised by their taste in wives. Richard, solid and dependable, had married a sweet and very pretty local girl, Daphne, whom he had doted on. William the younger, wilder and altogether more rakish son had decided his fortunes lay in finding a rich and glamorous American wife. Family tensions were compounded when, despite a blissfully happy marriage, Richard and Daphne had failed to produce an heir and instead adopted a baby boy from Belfast, little Rupert. Despite growing up into one of the loveliest and most charming men Jemima knew, Rupert Fairfax's childhood had been overshadowed by the fact that, as an adopted child, he couldn't inherit the title or break the ancient codicil which also prohibited him from inheriting the family estate. Matters came to a head one fateful day when, out hunting with his beloved hounds, Richard's horse failed to see a strand of wire atop a hedge and flipped, crushing him underneath. The horse staggered up and took itself home, but its rider had died instantly. Daphne was distraught, her nerves in tatters, and had never really recovered. Jessica, however, had taken the news very calmly from her Palm Beach home and within the week had packed up the household, and her young children, and flown back to take her place as chatelaine of Fairfax Park.

The bedroom Jemima stayed in was right next to Flora's, beautifully upholstered in duck egg blue, with a delicate mahogany four-poster bed and wide window looking down across the parkland out to sea. Someone had placed a hot water bottle underneath the sheets and a small fire was glowing in the grate. Jemima crossed to the window and peered out. The Fairfax land stretched all the way down to the sea, over the downs on which they would be hunting the next day, and when they had been little she and Flora had waited at the window to wave at the lights of the cargo ships miles offshore. She couldn't see any lights this evening. Someone had also laid out some riding clothes for Jemima; a neat jacket, well-polished boots, a shirt and stock, and a pair of jodhpurs which still carried the nametape FLORA FAIRFAX FORM 5. Jemima was looking forward to hunting tomorrow, although she hadn't been riding for a few years and couldn't help but be a bit nervous. She was also pessimistic about fitting in Flora's aged fourteen jodhpurs! Lord Fairfax had a particular interest in breeding his own hunters, who invariably were as glossy as conkers and utterly enormous – seventeen hands at least. If Jemima fell off tomorrow she was going to know about it – and she was not keen on spending her New Year in hospital, or worse, in a morgue – she had a diamond to deliver to Cape Town!

As she made her way back down to the kitchen, and a waiting glass of wine, she remembered John's hideous fur hat again. It suddenly came to her that she was sure she'd seen it on someone on Bond Street earlier that afternoon – she remembered wincing at the ugly colour of it. It was too much of a coincidence, there must be other hats like that in London, surely?

Chapter 7

Christmas Eve

When Jemima awoke early the next morning a silver veil of frost adorned the park outside her window, sparkling under a bright sun in a clear winter sky.

"It won't last," grumbled Lord Fairfax a little later, over an enormous breakfast of bacon, sausages, mushrooms, kippers, fried bread, devilled eggs, hash browns, roast tomatoes, porridge and croissants. Of course it was a small low-fat yoghurt for Lady Fairfax who was 'slimming'. Jemima eyed the spread over a coffee and wondered if she'd ever be able to get into Flora's old jodhpurs if she ate as much as she wanted to.

"Due heavy snow later," continued His Lordship over his newspaper. "We'll have to see where we are by about two-thirty, Henry. Don't want to be stuck out in a blizzard on Christmas Eve."

Henry looked up from his second helping of kedgeree

and nodded disinterestedly. He loved hunting – all the Fairfaxes did – but in his opinion, his father's undue concern for the welfare of his horses, hounds and guests hampered his day of sport.

There must have been thirty or forty horses at the meet by 11.30, milling around by the lake in front of the house. From her lofty perch atop an enormous bay mare, Jemima had quite a view. She was surreptitiously eyeing up a rather attractive huntsman whilst thinking how amazing it was that the scene hadn't changed much in over one hundred years. It was a magical sight. Henry, Flora and both their parents were all mounted up on Lord Fairfax's homebred horses – Lady Fairfax riding side-saddle in a particularly flashy habit with gold buttons, a full skirt and a nipped-in waist which looked gorgeously flamboyant, if a hundred and fifty years out of fashion. Jemima herself had been lent a huge bay mare called Bathsheba – Lord Fairfax was a big fan of Thomas Hardy – who she was relieved to find was incredibly gentle and sweet despite her size. Looking around, Jemima realised she couldn't see John, which didn't particularly surprise her – it was hard to imagine him near a horse, let alone hunting through muddy fields on one. She didn't know why she had this strange feeling about him. He'd been smarming away at breakfast to Lady Fairfax, who seemed desperate to get away from him, while Flora and Jemima caught each other's eyes and winced at each other every time he said something crass or rude.

Just then Rupert Fairfax, Flora and Henry's cousin,

sauntered over on his grey steed. He had always had a bit of a crush on Jemima – something she had done nothing but discourage, even though he was a sweet man. Short, ruddy and already balding, with a naughty merry glint in his eye, Rupert was as huge hearted as he was quick witted. Sometimes Jemima thought it a bit sad he wouldn't be able to inherit the estate he loved so much – the estate's tenants and the local villagers adored him, and he could be seen stomping around the fields and farms in all weathers in his shabby tweed coat, discussing drainage ditches, pheasant rearing and sheep with great enthusiasm. Henry, by contrast, preferred to hunt, shoot and fish in the privacy of the parkland, and rarely met the locals, except in the Fairfax Arms.

"Morning, Jemima, you're looking well, how are you?" Rupert rode up next to her and stood in the stirrups to peck her on the cheek. Despite having his pick of his uncle's shiny hunters, Rupert was very attached to his own horse, a short, skinny grey thoroughbred called Bostik. Bostik had previously been an abysmal racehorse but after romping home at the back of the field one time too many, his inebriated owner had stood on a chair in the racecourse bar and announced he'd swap the horse for a double gin and tonic. This could have gone badly for Bostik, but luckily Rupert was in the next seat along and took pity on him. Despite this inauspicious start, Bostik had paid Rupert back with utter devotion. Out hunting, he was the boldest and most careful jumper, spotting wire and rabbit holes, surefooted on any ground no matter how slippery or rugged, and taking huge hedges and yawning ditches in his stride.

"Rupes! I'm great – how are you? Where's your ma, not out?" Daphne, who was a fantastic horsewoman, was notably absent from the meet.

"Nope," said Rupert. "She's got her new boyfriend down and they've walked into the village to go to my grandparents' for coffee. Apparently," he leaned closer conspiratorially, "his daughter is coming down from London this afternoon. Mum's very star-struck."

"Oh? Who's his daughter?" Jemima was star struck on a daily basis in her job.

"Some actress called Melinda Jones?" said Rupert with a sideways look at Jemima.

Jemima raised an eyebrow. Melinda Jones was a gorgeous young film star, who'd most recently made an appearance as the latest Bond girl. Jemima had met her briefly before – for the latest première she had tried to get her to wear some Vogel jewellery, but she had charged so much that Mr V had refused, storming that she should be paying him and not the other way around. This tasty bit of information also meant that Daphne Fairfax's new boyfriend was Donald Jones Jr, the director of the latest remake of *To Catch a Thief*. Vogel in Monaco had lent some jewellery, and Jemima was hoping a trip to Cannes for the film festival the following year was on the cards when the movie was premièred.

"Who's that?" Rupert said sharply, looking behind Jemima.

She turned around and saw John coming towards them on foot holding a tray of mince pies and glasses of port.

"A friend of Henry's," she replied. "He's a bit odd."

"Is he now," muttered Rupert, eyeing him up and down. "He was stalking around the village very early this morning as I was taking the dogs for a walk – I don't usually see anyone else out at that time apart from Brian the milkman. He was skulking in the churchyard, looking distinctly dodgy so I asked him what he was doing and if I could help, and he said he was interested in the architecture – and was looking for the crypt. At five-forty-five in the morning? Bizarre. Anyway, I told him the only crypt around here was in the chapel here at Fairfax Park, not at St James's in the village. Oh, talking of – there's the Pip the Priest, I must go and say hello." Rupert rode off, just as John reached them with his tray.

"I thought that I'd help," he answered Jemima's surprised look, and proffered a glass of port. "Would you like one?"

"No thank you – I need to keep a clear head on this huge horse."

"Hang on, Johnno, I'll have one!" Henry rode up on his enormous horse, clearly already quite jolly. Jemima watched John hand Henry a glass of port, which he downed, then another one, and then take a hip flask from John and put it in his pocket. She hoped Henry wouldn't be stupid – she knew Granny Tinkerbell would be so angry if her grandson risked his neck drunk out hunting – she was already superstitious enough after the death of the last heir on a past Christmas Eve.

The hunting horn sounded, and Pip, the vicar of Fairfield appeared next to the Viscount to bless the hounds, huntsmen and horses. Lord Fairfax, looking resplendent in his scarlet hunting coat atop a huge dappled grey, was leaning down to give a final few instructions to the riders on the quadbikes who were setting the trail. When the vicar had done his duty, Viscount Fairfax sounded the horn and with that they were off, the first line taking them down the hill across the park from where the house stood. Jemima braced herself a little as she approached the first hedge, which loomed very large, but she dug in her heels and Bathsheba flew over it, barely breaking pace. A huge smile spread across Jemima's face – she'd forgotten how amazing this feeling was, the sound of hounds, the nip of the cold air on her face, the snorting of the horse underneath her and the sensation of flying as she took off for yet another jump. Coming up on her right, Flora caught up with her. "Great isn't it!" she called, and Jemima nodded. They galloped on, relieved to be out of the polluted London air and blowing away remnants of yesterday's martinis with the crisp sea air that was becoming increasingly close. The first line finished with a trot down a short track that opened out onto the Fairfax's private beach – a long stretch of glassy sand where Jemima let Bathsheba stretch out into a full gallop – racing Flora – before drawing rein on the sand dunes where the horses took a breath.

Henry rode over. Jemima hadn't seen much of him on the first line, although she'd heard him whooping as he jumped each jump and being sternly admonished by the joint master. Up close, he looked drunk to her – he was swaying slightly in the saddle and he sounded rather slurred.

"Bloody brilliant day isn't it?" he said cheerily just as the horn blew for the next line. "Tally ho!" With another whoop he'd clapped his legs to his horse's sides

"Hen – what's going on?" Flora screamed at him as he galloped off again away from them, behaving as though he was in the Grand National not out on a county hunt. But he obviously didn't hear. "Jemima, he's gone mad," Flora looked up at her friend. Underneath the flecks of mud her face had gone white. "I'm scared."

"I know he seems really pissed – but he's ridden this land all his life, I wouldn't worry," said Jemima, trying to sound convinced.

"So had Uncle Richard," Flora replied ominously. "I'm going to try and catch up with Daddy and warn him. If anyone can control him it'll be Pa."

"Or your mother," Jemima muttered under her breath.

The next line took them back up the hill away from the coast, parallel to the stone walls of Fairfax Park and through Fairfield village. It started to snow as they clattered through the hamlet, past the village green and the village church John had been hanging around that morning. Why had he been doing that, what utterly strange behaviour? thought Jemima. As they turned right and climbed another hill through a coppice the hounds lost the scent, and Flora and Jemima drew to a halt together to wait.

"Flora darling, have you seen Henry?" Lord Fairfax came cantering up.

"No. We thought he was up front with you!" replied Flora.

"That bloody boy!" said Lord Fairfax. "He's not here – probably buggered off to the pub as we went through the village. If he's left Captain Troy tied up outside and he catches a chill, I'll string him up!" He rode off, fuming.

"Oh, bloody hell that's all we need, Daddy in a bad mood for Mama's dinner," said Flora, sinking into her hunting jacket. "It's bloody freezing."

There was a pause, Jemima realised she couldn't feel her toes. The hounds were still running cheerily in circles.

"I'm going to head back, Flora. I'm catching hypothermia," she said, banging her hands against her thighs.

"Lucky you, I'm probably stuck here until Daddy decides it's time. Take the shortcut back past the chapel – you'll have to jump the gate back into the park but it's much quicker to get poor Sheba home." Bathsheba had started to shiver too.

Jemima turned her steed around and headed back to the stables past the chapel that stood on the outskirts of the estate. Built in the twelfth century, Fairfax Park's chapel had been near to where the original house had stood before it was demolished and taken further away from the village, up on the hill. It wasn't much in use these days, the villagers and most of the family used St James's in Fairfield village, but the chapel was still used for Fairfax family christenings, weddings and funerals – hatchings, matchings and dispatchings as Lord Fairfax, and *The Daily Telegraph*, called them. As she galloped past the tiny twelfth century building, she was sure she heard banging, and slowed her horse down to a walk, but as she got closer the sound died away. It was too cold to wait, beautiful as the tiny chapel looked under its light frosting of snow which was just starting to settle. She turned Bathsheba and headed home.

Chapter 8

Two o'clock in the afternoon

"Jemima, my dear, why are you back so early?" Granny Tinkerbell asked as Jemima walked into the huge kitchen from the stables, where the Dowager Viscountess was talking to the old cook Mrs Wright. "Is it snowing?"

"Just starting to settle. It was getting so cold I thought it was better to call it a day. Flora's still out, we think Henry's gone to the pub. I imagine everyone will be back soon."

"Good – you can come and chat with me in the drawing room. Wright, please bring us coffee, will you?"

Jemima followed the ninety-year-old Dowager out of the kitchen, across the huge galleried hall and into the drawing room, which had recently been reupholstered at great expense by a London interior designer, much to the old lady's chagrin.

"Oh, I'm a bit muddy, should I not…?"

"Oh no, don't worry about it! Jessica's upholstery needs a little wearing in!" she said with a wink.

Jemima sat down. Granny Tinkerbell assumed an expression of triumph as Jemima's muddy jodhpurs touched the hated blue chintz. Wright returned with a tray laden down with an enormous silver coffeepot, delicate china cups and saucers, and a pretty plate piled high with frangipane-topped mince pies.

"Thank you."

Jemima hadn't seen Granny Tinkerbell in a few years. The Dowager Viscountess, a former prima-ballerina, was known as Tinkerbell, thanks to her tiny frame and eponymous role in the 1948 ballet *Tinkerbell and Peter Pan*. She wanted to ask the old lady about the tiara – when she'd peeked at it in the hotel, the emeralds had been like nothing she had ever seen. And working at Vogel she wasn't short of experience with exceptional emeralds.

"Thinking about jewellery, dear?" Granny Tinkerbell smiled. Sometimes Jemima felt she could see right through her.

"Always. It was a gorgeous tiara we collected yesterday – amazing emeralds. Would it be a Fairfax family one?"

"I don't know – we do have a very beautiful, quite simple emerald one? My great aunt's wearing it in that portrait, so it's not strictly Fairfax but Bowes-Lyon." She gestured to an oil of a dark-haired beauty in a delicate emerald diadem. Jemima was impressed, she hadn't known Flora was essentially related to the Queen. The Queen Mother had been a Bowes-Lyon before she married the

Duke of York, who became George VI.

"I don't think it was that one. From what I could see in the dark bar at Claridge's, it was really quite large and ornate. There's a bandeau, about an inch high, with arches of white diamonds each surrounding a large pear-shaped emerald. Above this it looked like there were five large diamond six-point stars, with a large round emerald in the middle; the middle star is quite a bit bigger than the other four. It must be about four inches high at the front," Jemima explained and noticed the old lady's face relax in relief, smiling as though in the knowledge of something.

"Goodness me! No that doesn't sound like anything I have seen before, of ours or anyone else's, except..." Granny Tinkerbell thought for a moment. "Maybe something Barbara Hutton would have had made, or indeed Wallis Simpson! You do know that Jessica is a Woolworths heiress, Hutton was a much older cousin! That is where her money came from. In fact, as you can probably tell – she is spending a lot of it here." Granny Tinkerbell glowered at the new curtains as if they had committed her some great personal wrong.

"I just wondered because her ladyship had a valuation for the tiara in the box," said Jemima innocently.

"No!" Granny Tinkerbell whispered loudly in astonishment. "For how much?"

"I didn't dare open it – she would have seen the envelope seal broken and probably blamed Flora." It wasn't a secret that she was very harsh on her daughter.

"Quite right – but what a shame!" she giggled

mischievously. "Now. I want you to tell me about this Benjamin, Flora's boyfriend. Is he suitable for Flora? She has always been so wilful – I know mostly in rebellion to her mother."

"Oh, he's fine. Honestly, I really wouldn't worry – I used to go out with his brother, they're from a really lovely family, Benjy just doesn't want to follow the banking path."

"Well that is a relief. Thank you. Now what about you – you have a boyfriend? And how is work? Vogel wasn't it? I am afraid I don't really believe in buying new diamonds, after all we have more than enough in the Fairfax family vault here! As does Jessica it seems! Speaking of which – you know how Jessica likes us to dress up this evening – have you a tiara to wear?"

"No, but I have a very big yellow diamond ring!" Jemima suddenly remembered that in all the chaos of her arrival last night she'd left the diamond in her handbag instead of the safe as she'd intended, and mentally kicked herself. "I'm hoping that will suffice."

"I am not keen on coloured diamonds," she said rather snobbishly, and again Jemima couldn't help wonder if Julian Fellowes had modelled his Dowager Countess in *Downton Abbey* on her – after all he was a friend and neighbour of the Fairfaxes. "Let's go to the safe and pick something out for you. There are several Fairfax tiaras, some of which are very large – not as much as the one you have just described – created in the Victorian and Edwardian eras when they all wore huge pieces of jewellery, mainly for State occasions such as coronations. Sadly, we've all had to leave most of them in safes. But of course, tonight we can be as fancy as we like!"

The little fairy of a lady got up from her chair and motioned for Jemima to follow her. Jemima had visited Fairfax Hall since she was eight years old, when she and Flora were at prep school together, and she had thought that she knew the house pretty well. However, as she followed Granny Tinkerbell into the ancient and dusty library, she was surprised to find the old lady pushing open a door that had been concealed to look like a bookcase, and arriving in a room that Jemima had never known existed.

"No one comes in here usually," said Granny Tinkerbell. "So it will be very musty, but I know Jessica said that she was going to dig out some pieces for you and Flora to choose from this evening. Why don't we save her the trouble?" She winked at Jemima.

The room was musty and felt unused, but Jemima could sense that, despite Granny Tinkerbell's assertions, someone had been in there recently. She had an incredibly good sense of smell, and there was a faint odour of cigarettes and coffee in the air. The Viscountess? Perhaps she'd come to put away the tiara that they'd picked up from Garrard, but Jessica Fairfax didn't smoke and Jemima wondered when she would have had time to travel to this remote part of the house to deposit the piece she was no doubt wearing later that night.

The old lady made her way over to what looked like a

large portrait sketch by Rubens.

"Is that a…?"

"Yes," she replied as she looked back at Jemima with a smile. "It was in my family. I wanted to have it in my room, but my son thought it wasn't safe to have it there, so it's here until I die! I'm leaving it to Flora, but you mustn't tell her." The enormous portrait turned out to be on a very well-balanced runner – tiny Granny Tinkerbell slid it and its frame back with little effort to reveal a safe door. She twisted the lock twice and the door clicked open, but she had difficulty in opening the heavy door.

"I'll do it." Jemima moved forward and pulled it open. The safe went a long way back and was divided into different sections. There were lots of files and ancient documents, and a small stack of jewellery boxes in all sizes – from big enough to fit a bowling ball in to tiny little cases that contained just a ring.

"There are five Fairfax tiaras – shall we have a look at them? I think she will probably want Flora to wear that one." She pointed to a large navy leather case. Jemima pulled it out and they put it on the table against the wall. "Go on, open it."

Jemima had just flicked the catches on the box when her phone rang. It was Flora.

"Hi, are you on your way back?" she asked her friend.

"We're all back at the stables, the hounds have gone back to the kennels. The snow started coming down hard and it was too thick to carry on. Have you seen Henry? He didn't reappear. Probably still at the pub. But my parents are a bit concerned with this lack of visibility."

"Oh gosh – no he's not with us. I'm with your grandmother choosing a tiara!"

"Typical! He'll be back soon I'm sure. We'll be back in five minutes, come to the kitchen – Wright will have made tea."

She hung up and told the old lady, whose face immediately went white.

"He's met the same fate as my poor Richard," she whispered.

"No, no," said Jemima reassuringly. "He's just gone off drinking with his friend John – no one could get hold of him either."

Granny Tinkerbell still looked worried. Jemima picked up the box containing the tiara for Flora, and Granny Tinkerbell handed her another three cases – a tiara for Jemima, and necklaces and earrings for them both – and locked the safe up again.

They went through the big hall on the way to the kitchen but were stopped by Daphne and her boyfriend.

"Oh, my dear," Granny Tinkerbell cried when Daphne greeted her. "We're terrified that Henry has met the same fate as Richard." Daphne looked shocked.

"No, we're not," said Flora, who stomped in looking bedraggled. "I'm sure he's fine. He's just playing silly buggers."

"Why don't we have a cup of tea?" suggested Jemima, sensing the tension brewing.

"I think I need something stronger," Flora said

stomping off towards the drawing room where there was a very well stocked drinks cabinet.

"I am going to go and change out of this wet hunting garb. And I suggest you do too, Flora." The elegant and tall Viscountess, her blonde hair still immaculate after hours in a riding hat, called after her daughter. "I don't want you getting drunk all afternoon and not be able to sit down for dinner tonight."

"If there is a tonight. You can't expect us to have the grand dinner if something is wrong with Henry," whispered Granny Tinkerbell.

"We will dress and sit down for dinner as is tradition," said Viscountess Fairfax firmly. Jemima bit her lip and tried not to laugh at the expression of outrage that had briefly crossed Granny Tinkerbell's face – she had looked moments away from telling Jessica that it had not been a tradition while her husband was alive. "I am certain that Henry will be back soon," continued Jessica. "Has anyone called the village pub? And where on earth is that friend of his?" She swept off up the huge sweeping staircase.

Chapter 9

Three o'clock in the afternoon

While Granny Tinkerbell was comforted by her favourite daughter-in-law, Flora headed over to the drinks tray and mixed up an enormous jug of Bloody Mary cocktail.

Jemima, who was back with the others after depositing the evening's elegant jewels in her room under the bed, turned to Daphne's boyfriend, the famous film director, who'd been hovering awkwardly in the doorway. "Hello, I'm Jemima Fox-Pearl," she said, sitting herself down on the blue chintz sofa she'd been perched on earlier, and trying to limit the spread of mud from her hunting clothes. She wished she'd been able to bathe and change before meeting him – he must have been twenty years older than Jemima but was still absurdly attractive. A kind of older Brad Pitt. "You must be Donald Jones. I gather that you directed the remake of *To Catch a Thief*? I'm head of PR at Vogel Diamonds – we lent the jewellery for the film. I'm so excited to see it on the big screen."

At the mention of his film, Donald warmed. "Oh, yes I know – beautiful pieces! We're having a big premiere in Monaco to open the Cannes Film Festival in May – I'm hoping Glenn and Evie will be borrowing some more from you. Oh, and my producer, Fortunata Lindberg."

"I'm sure that will be possible," smiled Jemima, she'd always wanted to meet Glenn Close. "And your daughter Melinda is in the movie I think?"

"Yes, yes she is. She couldn't make it down today unfortunately or she'd have been at dinner with us. Her train from London was cancelled."

"Oh, what a shame!" Rupert would be disappointed! "So, are you allowed to tell me what you're working on now?"

"Yes, actually! *Thief* gave me a taste for jewellery heists, so the next film is going to be based around one of them," he said. This clearly caught Granny Tinkerbell's attention, because she broke off from her conversation with Daphne and looked over.

Flora, who was passing around Bloody Marys joined in, "Jem's company has had quite a lot of heists over the years, hasn't it?"

"Well yes – I suppose it has," said Jemima. "They all have though – the big Bond Street jewellers. The Pink Panther gang alone has stolen close to a billion pounds over the past fifteen years."

"At the moment we're interested in historical ones," said Donald. "I'm actually over here researching the famous theft of Wallis Simpson's jewels after World War Two."

"I can tell you all about that," said Tinkerbell, brightening up suddenly.

"How come, Granny?"

"Well, I was there."

Chapter 10

Four o'clock tea time

"**S**Hush, everyone! Granny is going to tell us about when the Crown Jewels were stolen!" said Flora, as her mother came into the drawing room and announced that tea was ready in the small dining room. Her guests dutifully started to get up.

"Flora, this is really not the time for such stories," snapped Jessica. "Wright and the kitchen staff are waiting for us for tea in the small dining room so that they can get on with tonight's dinner."

"We'll carry on with Christmas dinner tonight?" enquired her mother-in-law again. "Even if Henry isn't found or indeed it is worse than that?"

"Henry will be found," said Jessica irritably. "William has gone down to the village to retrieve him. It's just taking a little while because of the snow. Honestly, I'm furious – going AWOL on today of all days."

Outside Jemima noticed the snow was getting thicker

– she couldn't even make out the obelisk at the edge of the lake any more, and it was starting to settle in drifts around the windowsill.

"Oh, come on then. Granny, you can tell us the story over tea," said Flora, getting up and heading towards the dining room.

The table was beautifully laid with a sumptuous array of finger sandwiches, such as egg mayonnaise, tomato and cucumber; small pastries and cakes sat elegantly on stands, an immense Victoria sponge cake was formidably placed on a large china plate in the middle of the table and the thinnest of Spode china cups and saucers perfectly matched the tiny plates which indicated each placement. Decoration was provided by bowls of figs, dates and caramelised almonds sitting amidst holly and ferns which were strewn amongst the delicacies. Rupert had sidled in just as everyone else arrived and had seated himself next to Jemima. As instructed by their hostess, everyone helped themselves and once they all had food on their plates, Granny Tinkerbell sat up even straighter than her ballerina's posture should allow, and began to tell the story.

"It was the autumn of 1946 when it happened – I was expecting Richard at the time. Your great-grandmother, Flora, was appalled that I should be seen with Royalty when I had a protruding stomach. Although everyone despised Wallis, David – once Edward VIII – was still very much loved. He had after all been our King, albeit for a very short time."

She paused for a sip of lapsang souchong tea.

"David was so charming and still well-loved amongst our friends, even though there had been lots of rumours floating around about him befriending and helping Hitler. They did think it was under her persuasion." Granny Tinkerbell made a face.

"I had met them in Paris earlier that year, just after we were married, and they had returned from the Bahamas. At the time I was dancing Princess Aurora as Margot Fonteyn's understudy in *Sleeping Beauty* – did you know I used to be a ballerina, Donald? – and the Windsors requested we perform for them at their mansion in the Bois de Boulogne. Madame Fonteyn couldn't – or rather wouldn't – go, so I went instead. She suddenly treated me as a needed friend, after that trip. David had been friends with my father-in-law, he was your grandfather's godfather." She looked at Flora.

There was another pause while Tinkerbell delicately took a mouthful of her cucumber sandwich. "When they eventually came over that autumn – for what was her first visit to England since his abdication and their subsequent marriage in 1937 – they borrowed Ednam Lodge in Sunningdale from the Earl of Dudley. They had to – they weren't allowed to stay in any of the palaces, you see. It caused quite a scandal at the time. Wallis arrived with lorry loads of clothes and belongings, and what with the country on rations and essentially penniless after the war, she put quite a few noses out of joint I can tell you. And of course, she came bedecked in many of the jewels that David had lavished on her. Jewels were her passion – she had so many and was rarely seen in the same pieces more than once!"

"Richard bought me a beautiful amethyst necklace as my wedding present at the Geneva auction of her jewellery," interrupted Daphne. "Do you remember, Tinkerbell, we went together?"

"Of course. Quite a few of her jewels have been sold at auctions over the years," said the Dowager Viscountess. "Jemima dear, didn't Sidney Vogel buy her emerald engagement ring?"

"No, Lady Fairfax, that was Laurence Graff – he gave it to his wife. But Mr Vogel did buy a few other pieces of hers."

"Go on, Granny – finish your story," Flora urged.

"Well, Hector and I drove down from town to Sunningdale the day after the robbery – we'd arranged to have tea with them that day at Claridge's, but both the Windsors and Dudleys had left London straight after it had happened, so David asked if we'd come to Ednam instead. I think he'd hoped to distract Wallis, but it was incredibly distressing. She had been so rude to Laura Dudley's staff, accusing them all in turn of stealing the jewellery, and left us all standing for hours in the hall while she berated the cook – I was pregnant don't forget and poor Hector was having to practically hold me up by the time we finally sat down. David couldn't stop apologising."

"Who took the jewels, and did they ever find any of the pieces?" Jemima said, fascinated. It was like something out of an Agatha Christie.

"A full list of jewellery was released by Scotland Yard with the offer of a reward, but the Duchess hinted that there were pieces not included on it. I never found out what. The following day someone found the jewellery box on the golf course near hole five, with several pieces strewn around it – including a very valuable pearl necklace which once belonged to Queen Alexandra, David's grandmother."

"But who stole them and how?" Rupert asked, now stuffing his mouth full of Victoria sponge cake.

"That is what is so strange. No one was ever caught! They did eventually arrest someone who already had a recently new record of petty thievery, and jailed him for it – although he never admitted. There were lots of conspiracy theories, although I can't remember the exact details. The Royal Family weren't happy about Wallis having so many expensive jewels, you see."

"Conspiracy theories. Like what?!"

"Enough, Flora," her mother almost bellowed down the table. "Your grandmother said that she can't remember."

If Lady Fairfax wasn't so annoyed at Henry's absence, Jemima would have been surprised at her reaction. She was always a little abrupt and harsh with her daughter, but today it was on a whole new level, particularly about the jewellery. And the mutual dislike between the two viscountesses was not a secret, but it seemed that she really wasn't interested in hearing the story – when it was such a scandal.

"And don't forget the emeralds," the film director piped up, ignoring his hostess.

"What emeralds?" Flora gasped.

"Oh well, that was one of the conspiracy theories," he continued, noticing Jessica Fairfax redden. "Apparently amongst the jewels that went missing were emeralds that had belonged to your Queen Alexandra. The one whose pearls were found on the links."

"Why was it a conspiracy theory?" Jemima asked.

"No one really knew if David had given Wallis the emeralds, or indeed if they ever really existed – they've never been seen since. It was thought that David's grandmother, the Danish Queen Alexandra, was given a set of enormous uncut emeralds by her sister, Minnie – Empress Maria Feodorovna of Russia," explained Tinkerbell. "These emeralds were vastly valuable, and most royals thought such important jewels should be kept within the family. For a while their potential status was the subject of some debate. It is thought that Alexandra left them to her grandson in her personal will – which would have meant that they were not, in fact, part of the Crown Jewels but private items," explained Tinkerbell. "If that was the case then Edward was able to do what he liked with them – give then to Wallis Simpson for example." Jemima couldn't help noticing that she glanced over at her daughter-in-law, the current Viscountess, before pausing and looked at the film director.

"However, as I am sure you have learnt through your research, Mr Jones, there were two schools of thought about what happened to such valuable jewels, if they did exist. Most think that either the Royal Family, the Queen Mother – then Queen Elizabeth – most particularly, planned the burglary to steal them back. Or that it was an inside job by the Windsors themselves, for the insurance money of the rest of Wallis's jewel case, and as a cover up to vanish the emeralds under the Royal Family's noses. Only £25,000 was claimed, but it was clear from the list that much more than that was stolen, particularly if it included the historic Russian emeralds."

"This is thrilling. Your movie will be amazing, darling. You should get Tinkerbell to be an advisor!" laughed Daphne, happy that her mother-in-law seemed to like her new boyfriend.

"Flora, no more wine – you have had quite enough already," Lady Fairfax suddenly interrupted. "I told you not to drink too much before tonight. Don't forget that we'll be meeting in the drawing room at 7pm." And at that she rose angrily from her chair, rang a small bell to summon the staff to clear away the tea and stalked out. Everyone followed suit, reluctantly finishing off the last of their delicious cakes. Outside, the snow whirled down.

"I hope Henry's back before too long," said Flora as she and Jemima climbed the staircase. Jemima couldn't wait to get out of her hunting gear. "It's unusual for him to miss the Christmas Eve tea, and the snow's getting so heavy." She yawned staring out of one of the huge windows on the staircase. "I'm going up for a bath and a nap."

"I think I'll probably do the same," said Jemima. Her mind was racing – she wanted to be alone in her room to look up the Windsor's jewellery heist and check that the Vogel diamond ring was still in her bag. The story of the Windsor emeralds absolutely fascinated her, and she thought that she must have a contact somewhere who'd be able to tell her more. The more she thought about what Rupert had told her at the meet, the more she was also starting to become convinced that the person following her and Flora down Bond Street had been Henry's strange friend John. But what did he want? And where did he fit into all this.

Chapter 11

Six o'clock in the evening

t was pitch black outside when the snow finally stopped falling at 6pm. Jemima lay in a hot bubble bath, already feeling stiff from riding after so long, and mustering the energy to get out of the deliciously warm water and dress for dinner. She'd tried to sleep, especially as she could hear Flora snoring in the next room, but her head was so full of jewellery heists and strangers following her down Bond Street she couldn't settle. Hoisting herself out of the deep and ancient looking bath, she dried her aching body with a large but not particularly fluffy white towel and sat on the end of the tub to rub in the rose scented Crabtree & Evelyn crème Lady Fairfax had left for her guests.

She had already opened the green leather case containing one of the Fairfax tiaras that she was borrowing for the evening. It had turned out to be the one Tinkerbell's Great Aunt had been wearing in the oil painting in the drawing room – it had old mine cut diamonds set in Edwardian scrollwork design, with what looked like an eight-carat cabochon emerald suspended in the centre.

Emeralds are not particularly hardy gemstones, which is why they're not often used as engagement rings, and despite this tiara having been exceptionally well looked after, Jemima could tell it was at least a hundred years old and had seen quite a lot of wear in its time. However, other than the gemstones being emeralds and diamonds, it was completely dissimilar to the one that she taken a quick look at the previous evening when she was waiting for Flora in the Claridge's bar, which had looked much newer and less worn.

Jemima began mulling over the enormous tiara they'd picked up from Garrard. If Tinkerbell didn't recognise it, it must be one of Jessica's own, which would make sense. Jemima had known that Jessica Fairfax was somehow related to the Woolworth family – the same family who founded the chain of shops that appeared on every high street in England. She and Flora had laughed every time they saw one when they were little. The Woolworths had been vastly, unimaginably rich at the start of the twentieth century. Upon his death in 1919 the founder of the company, Frank Winfield Woolworth, had been a multi-billionaire in modern money, owning a measurable amount of the GNP of the whole of America. His granddaughter, the tragic socialite and heiress Barbara Hutton, had accumulated over a billion dollars of inheritance by her twenty-first birthday in 1933. Even a tiara as big as the one from Garrard would have been a mere trinket to the Woolworths. As she wrapped herself in her dressing gown and started blow-drying her hair, Jemima wondered how exactly Jessica was related to them. After a moment, curiosity overcame her, and she put the dryer down again and picked up her phone.

The Wi-Fi signal, notoriously bad in old large houses, took ages to load and there was no phone signal out here in the middle of the sticks. Nevertheless, after a few false attempts Jemima managed to bring up an announcement in *The Daily Telegraph* archives of Flora's parents wedding. Viscountess Fairfax had been Jessica McCann then, and the article described her as, 'Great-great-granddaughter of Woolworths founder Frank Winfield Woolworth, and much younger cousin of socialite Barbara Hutton.' Perhaps it was Barbara who left her the tiara – after all, Jemima read, Barbara had only had one child, a son who had predeceased her, dying tragically in a plane crash in 1972. With no daughters to pass the tiara on to, maybe Barbara had entailed it to Jessica?

Still mulling it over, Jemima finished drying her hair, dabbed on a little Chanel No. 5 and began applying her make-up. Entailing jewellery that valuable to a cousin would have been an unusual move though, thought Jemima. The tiara's huge! Frowning, she opened her phone again and typed in a few more phrases. Jessica McCann, it seemed, had been named after Jessie Donahue, her grandmother's sister, who herself had once had an astounding jewellery collection. Quickly she typed in 'Jessie Donahue Jewellery' and then when that didn't yield any results 'Jessie Donahue Tiara'. Bingo! Up popped a photo of a New York ball in 1952, and with a flash of excitement Jemima realised that the tiara the woman in the middle of the photograph was wearing was the one she'd caught a glimpse of in the case at Claridge's! But wait, Jemima's heart leapt as she scanned the photograph, enlarged it, and looked again at the faces of the photograph's subjects. There was Jessie Donahue alright, standing to the left of the group, but she was wearing a simple diamond circlet. Jemima realised with a shock that the woman in the middle of the photograph wearing the enormous emerald and diamond tiara Flora had picked up from Garrards, was none other than the Duchess of Windsor.

Jemima sat down on the bed and thought fast. Why had Wallis Simpson been wearing Jessie Donahue's tiara? And why on earth had Jessica Fairfax been getting the tiara valued at Garrards? The emeralds in it alone must have been worth a fortune, but the Fairfaxes didn't need the money. Emeralds… thought Jemima. Something stirred in her memory. She thought of the story of the theft of the Duchess of Windsor's jewels, of the rumour that a set of uncut emeralds had been stolen too. But the emeralds in the tiara were cut, and brilliantly so. It would be too much to imagine that they were the same stones wouldn't it?

Jemima pulled up Google again, located a newspaper archive website and started scrolling through pages of information and newspaper articles from October 1946.

The jewellery robbery was front page news on most. Some of them mentioned the rumour of emeralds but said that they didn't appear on the official list, and therefore had probably never existed. Flicking forward a few weeks, she located the coverage of the trial. A man called Leslie Holmes had been imprisoned for the theft, she found, although he had never admitted to it. Another article, a few years on, mentioned that the detective in charge of the case had visited him in prison and each Christmas sent a card. She read on and suddenly sat bolt upright. The officer in question was one Detective Insp. John Capstick of Scotland Yard. John Capstick. She was sure Henry's friend's surname was Capstick. That was too much of a coincidence – were they related? There had to be a connection.

Brimming over with questions, Jemima glanced at her bedside clock and realised that she was supposed to be down in the hall for drinks in ten minutes – and she was still standing stark naked. Pulling on a trusty gold and green finely knitted dress, that she had found in a sale in New Look years before (a favourite of Jemima's which looked a mixture between a Missoni and a 1920s style, had seen her through several wild parties, and never failed to look the most expensive thing in the room despite its discount price tag) and a pair of strappy shoes, she secured the pretty Edwardian emerald and diamond tiara to her head. She was pleased that Vogel store director Charles Fenwick had shown her how to put a tiara on properly one day before a fashion shoot, especially as her freshly-washed hair had very little grip. She slipped the Vogel yellow diamond ring on to the right fourth finger as she left her room, hurrying along the corridors hoping to grab Flora for a word before cocktails.

Walking along the gallery above the hall however, she could hear pandemonium downstairs. Stepping downstairs as fast as her heels would allow, she found Jessica crying hysterically in the middle of the hall, fully made up with her hair in rollers, wearing a silk dressing gown and velvet slippers, leaning on Wright for support while Lord Fairfax stood at the other end of the hall, still in his hunting gear, red in the face and bellowing.

"Fuck your bloody tiara, I've lost my son!"

"Flora!" said Jemima as she tottered to the bottom of the stairs. "What's happened?"

Flora was white. "Mama's tiara has gone. The one that we collected last night."

"What?"

"It's not just that," Flora gulped. "Henry's still missing but they've… they've found his horse."

Rupert appeared with a whisky for Lady Fairfax and helped Wright seat her in a low pink damask silk Louis XIV chair. She was still sobbing about her tiara, and Jemima could hear her blaming the entire household, including her mother-in-law and Daphne, for its loss.

"What happened?" said Jemima, as Rupert walked over to them.

"Terrible business," said Rupert. "Did Flora tell you about the horse? Been shot. Looks like a rifle, someone hit him through the chest as he was coming over a hedge a few fields over from where we were – the horse crumpled on landing and must have thrown Henry. What the stupid bugger was doing that far away from the rest of the field I have no idea, but he was pissed, and I suppose he wanted to get a few extra jumps in."

"Where's Henry then?" said Jemima, unable to believe her ears.

"We don't know," said Rupert grimly. "The police are out in a helicopter – that's how they found the horse, but the snow's so thick they can't see much."

"There's something else," said Flora. "His friend's still not back. The police are looking for him now, they think he's involved. That he's kidnapped Henry."

"But he's Henry's friend? He wouldn't do a thing like that," said Jemima, somewhat unsure of what she was saying.

"I don't think he is – Henry's only known him a few months," said Jemima. "He invited him to stay for Christmas because this John fellow seems to have spun him a yarn about being an orphan and lonely at Christmas, and you know what Henry's like."

"Flora," said Jemima suddenly, "do you remember what John's surname was?"

"What? No?" said Flora surprised. "It was something like Lipstick wasn't it?"

"Yes! I was right – it was Capstick, you thought it was Chapstick!"

"What are you on about, Jem?" Flora looked annoyed.

"My brother's out in the snow somewhere and you're—"

Jemima interrupted, "John Capstick was the police officer in charge of the theft of the Duchess of Windsor jewels in 1946 – the jewels that went missing were never found, but there's a theory the emeralds—"

"Fuck the emeralds!" shouted Flora, sounding suddenly very like her father.

"Flora's right, Jem," said Rupert kindly as he saw Jemima retreat suddenly at her friend's rebuke. "We can talk about jewel thieves another time. The important thing is finding Henry, and we don't even know where to start. "

Something clicked in Jemima's mind, and she gasped. "Yes we do – the chapel."

Rupert looked confused. "Chapel? What's the chapel got to do with this?"

"You saw John skulking round St James's this morning, didn't you?" said Jemima quickly. "But he was looking for a crypt, and you said St James's doesn't have one, but there is one…"

"At the chapel on the edge of the estate," breathed Flora. "But how are we going to get there? The snow's too deep to drive."

Rupert looked up. "I've got an idea."

Chapter 12

Ten o'clock at night

Jemima, Flora and Rupert sprinted through the house. Lord Fairfax followed behind, shouting into his mobile phone, "The crypt, man! The crypt, at the east edge of the estate. If they follow the estate wall towards the village, it's near the crossroads. Land on the north side – everything else is graveyard. No, I don't care how they do it, just get them there!"

"What's happening with the chopper, Uncle William?" said Rupert.

"The police are coming, but the helicopter's been out all afternoon and it needs to refuel, particularly as they'll need to use the blades to blow enough snow off the ground to land. They're heading back to Bournemouth – it'll be a forty-minute turnaround minimum."

"What!" said Flora aghast. "But what about Henry? He's stuck in the crypt with a madman!"

"The police say there's no proof of that – they're still

treating it as a missing persons case – they're sending officers in cars to continue in the meantime," said Lord Fairfax grimly.

"But with the snow they could be hours!" said Jemima.

"I know," said Lord Fairfax. "We need to get to the crypt. Rupert?"

Rupert looked up. "I'm going to need to borrow Bostik."

"Bostik?" said Flora. "What's he got to do with this, Daddy?"

"He'll be quicker across ground than a car will in these conditions. I'll take him and get to the chapel first, find Henry. Flora and Rupert, take the smaller tractor and go around by the road – tow any struggling police you see and make sure you block all the exit routes down to the village."

As he spoke, he opened the gun safe and took out two guns, passing one to Flora. "We know he's armed. You're a better shot than Rupert." Flora nodded and pulled a tweed coat on over her evening dress.

"Jemima, I'll need you to come with me – there's clearly something dodgy going on with this John fellow, and I agree with you that it's caught up with this tiara."

Jemima's face betrayed her surprise – she hadn't even known Lord Fairfax had taken an interest in his wife's jewellery, much less that someone else might share her theories about the tiara.

"Don't look so shocked – I'm not stupid. There's something wrong about that piece of jewellery, always has been ever since my wife picked it up off the Astors' yacht at Poole Marina. Capstick must have taken it. I'll need your knowledge in case we manage to talk him around."

In under three minutes, Jemima was scrambling onto Bathsheba's broad back, fingers already going numb on the reins. She'd handed her enormous Vogel ring and the Fairfax tiara she'd been wearing to Andrews the butler, who'd appeared at His Lordship's elbow like a perfectly punctual shadow. He presented her with a pair of overalls, which she'd pulled on over her dress, and her own Dior moonboots – which Flora must have nicked from Jemima's London flat for her latest skiing holiday. If we ever get out of this mess, I'll buy Flora a pair of her own, thought Jemima grimly. Lord Fairfax appeared, leading Bostik and holding two large lights. "We use them for lambing," he explained. "Strap it to your chest, it's pitch black out there." He mounted Bostik and rode out of the yard into the dark snow.

"Follow Bostik," he said firmly. "Sheba's a good girl, but Bostik's more surefooted – he'll be the first to see anything." He spurred Bostik into a trot, and then a slow canter. Jemima followed, holding tightly into Bathsheba's mane, and giving the horse her head to balance herself.

It was eerily silent. Every now and then, their lamps would catch the eyes of some nocturnal animal making their way through the snow, who would stop and stare with eyes like mirrors. As they neared the estate wall the wind had blown the snow up into drifts three or four feet deep and they had to slow down to a walk to let the horses pick their way through. The snow was deep enough to touch the top of Jemima's moonboots. She shivered as snow dripped down inside. What kind of state would Henry be in when they found him in these temperatures? she wondered.

"Nearly there," grunted Lord Fairfax. The snow was balling up in the horses' feet, and they were struggling through as the drifts got deeper. "One last…" he tailed off. In front of them yawned the River Fairbourne. Perhaps thirty feet wide, the river was passable, but it was deep enough for the horses to have to swim, and icy cold.

"Perhaps there's another way around?" suggested Jemima.

"It'll take too long," said Lord Fairfax. "We can't jump hedges in the dark, and the next gate's half a mile down the estate wall. It would take ages for the horses to struggle down there – we don't have time."

Jemima groaned inwardly at what was coming. Spurring Bostik on, Lord Fairfax held the lamp and his gun over his head to keep them dry and rode into the river. Jemima followed. The cold made Bathsheba snort, and Jemima gave a lurch and nearly slipped as the horse kicked off from the bottom. Icy water came over Jemima's legs, up to her navel – it was freezing. She managed to whip the lamp around her chest up into the air just as another rush of water came over her and then, just as quickly as it had started, it was over, and they were on the other side. Bostik shook himself like a dog. They turned and headed towards the chapel, and Jemima realised her hunch had been right –

in the window of the rarely used chapel shone a single light in the darkness. There was someone in there.

They dismounted at the lychgate where they left the horses in the shelter, and Jemima followed Lord Fairfax through the snow, which was getting deeper as they reached the gothic building. Jemima's moonboots, soaked from their dip in the Fairbourne, were icy, icy cold and heavy. They reached the door, and as Lord Fairfax twisted the handle, they realised it was already open. Inside the church was musty – sheets covered the pews and some of the marble statues, and someone had spread newspaper on the stone floor to catch a patch of pigeon droppings. It was damp and cold.

"No one's been in here for a year at least," murmured Lord Fairfax. "The last family occasion was a funeral about eighteen months ago."

"Someone's definitely been in here tonight," said Jemima, nodding towards the lamp that had been left on the altar. "That was the light we could see from the window."

"But where are they now?"

"The crypt!" she said, and then wished she hadn't. Why had she come on this 007'esque mission – she was terrified of the idea of an underground crypt.

"Yes, of course!" said William, and led them through thick snow to the back of the chapel and another oak door, which was a little bit ajar. Taking a deep breath for her nerves, Jemima followed him down the dark and steep stone steps, dreading what they'd find. It was particularly damp in the crypt, and Jemima's frozen feet slipped a little on the slimy floor. She heard a click, nearly walked into the back of Lord Fairfax, and looked up. There, amongst the sarcophagi was John Capstick, holding a gun.

Chapter 13

Fairfax Chapel crypt
11 o'clock at night

"What have you done with my son?" roared Lord Fairfax, seemingly unconcerned by the pistol that was now weaving figures of eight in the air in front of a shaking Capstick. Lord Fairfax's own gun was still slung uselessly across his back. Jemima had already seen Henry however. He was lying in a crumpled heap at the bottom of one of the tombs, barely breathing.

"He's, he's alive," said Capstick in a shaking voice. Jemima moved towards Henry, and Capstick didn't stop her. Henry was cold, with a bruise on his temple and his breath coming short and shallow.

"Why did you do this?" she asked, but she'd already seen the jewels, lying glittering in a dirty red canvas sports bag – some of the most beautiful jewels Jemima had ever seen in real life.

"Where did you find all this jewellery?" demanded Lord Fairfax. "Whose is it? And where is my wife's tiara?"

"I – I don't know anything about a tiara…" stuttered Capstick, gun still trembling in front of him. He feared the gun he was holding, Jemima realised, this man was not a killer.

"But man, whose is this jewellery? My wife's?" roared Lord Fairfax, still apparently completely unconcerned that he was being held at gunpoint by a man who in all probability had just kidnapped his son.

Capstick looked blank for a moment and then, slowly, lowered the ancient looking pistol.

"The man who buried them here sent a confession to my grandfather on his deathbed." He leant heavily against a tomb and looked at Jemima.

"It was my grandfather who told me all about the case of the Duchess of Windsor's stolen jewels when I was a child. He was Detective Inspector John Capstick, of Scotland Yard."

Jemima sucked in her breath – she'd been right.

He paused, before continuing, "I found the confession last year. My father had died, and I was sorting through his belongings. Amongst my father's papers was an old letter, unopened, addressed to my grandfather at Scotland Yard. Why my father had kept it and not opened it, I don't know."

Out of his coat pocket he pulled some sheets of what Jemima could see was blue Basildon Bond writing paper, on which was barely legible writing. "It tells everything.

How he, a Leslie Holmes that is, was contacted about carrying out the theft on 11 October 1946, just after the Duke and Duchess of Windsor arrived in England from Paris. How he had been hired to steal some large green stones by a man in a dark suit he had met in the pub. How he knew it was dangerous, but he was desperate – he'd been left unable to work after the terrors he saw in the war and had nothing else. He had no idea how his 'boss' had discovered him, but the money was good – enough to support his family for a few years even. He says in this letter, that they never contacted him again – a real one-off job." Capstick was now turning the letter over in his fingers.

"He got into the Duchess's bedroom at Ednam Lodge, took the jewel box and once out on the golf course, far enough away from the house he prised it open. But the jewels he was required to steal, namely loose green stones, were not there. So, he took these instead." John pointed to the bag open next to him, in which gemstones in every colour glittered.

"Wallis Simpson's missing jewellery," Jemima whispered, reaching down and pulling the bag towards her. She recognised their style from the 1987 Sotheby's catalogue of the sale of the Duchess of Windsor's jewels after her death, and the plethora of jewellery books which contained photos of her, which Jemima had spent years flicking through. There were at least a dozen pieces of what looked like Cartier and Van Cleef, which wasn't surprising – they were famously the Duchess's favourite jewellers. There was a white diamond brooch in the shape of a beautiful bird, several diamond and aquamarine pieces including a bracelet and a huge solitaire ring, and another huge solitaire ring in the form a very big square cut emerald. "But why are they here?"

"It's all here." He waved the letter again. "The thief, Leslie Holmes, travelled down to visit a cousin who lived in Fairfield. Eric Holmes."

"Aah yes, I remember him – he died recently. Used to work on the estate, like his father before him." Lord Fairfax nodded, seemingly calmer.

"He spent his childhood holidays here, he knew the crypt and decided to bury the jewels until he could come back and get them. But he never did. He was too worried about being caught, after being imprisoned for some other smaller thefts."

"So, you decided to steal these jewels back and, on the way, you just thought you'd take a potshot at my son, hey?" snarled Lord Fairfax, who didn't seem to be calming down after all. Capstick didn't move. Jemima noticed for the first time in the gloom that John wasn't wearing his badly fitting tweed suit, but a black tracksuit with a hood. What looked like a balaclava was poking out of his pocket.

"I – I didn't mean to," said Capstick.

"I'll have you charged with attempted murder!" shouted Lord Fairfax. Jemima put a hand on his arm. "And that was my great grandfather's duelling pistol. You stole it from the safe room."

"Why did you shoot Henry's horse, John?" she asked

quietly, realising why the room behind the bookcase smelled of smoke and coffee.

"Henry told me about the old guns in the car." He coughed. "I was going to the crypt while you were all out hunting," said Capstick. "I thought it would be the best time to check. I was wearing black, and a balaclava – I didn't want to be recognised if I was caught going through the crypt. I was crossing the field when Henry came up behind me – he was drunk and didn't recognise me. He thought I was trying to disrupt the hunt and started riding after me, shouting that it was a drag hunt, that it was legal, and I should get off his land. I didn't know what to do so I tried to fire a shot past him to scare him off from behind a hedge, but I couldn't see what I was doing. I hit the horse as it jumped the hedge and it threw Henry. It knocked him out, so I dragged him down here, to try and think of what to do next, but then we got snowed in."

"A fluke of a fucking shot," William Fairfax said sadly. "There must have been a bullet left inside. Those pistols haven't ever been used in my lifetime."

Just then they heard voices outside, and the whump, whump sound of a helicopter coming into land. Flora and Rupert, thought Jemima, and the police! Capstick looked frozen to the spot. She could hear footsteps crunching in the snow, and then Flora shouting, "The crypt's down here!" Crash! The door behind Lord Fairfax flew open, and there stood Flora, loaded shotgun in her hands pointing down the stone stairs. Behind her stood a very worried Armed Response Police Officer.

"I really can't let you point that at anyone, Honourable Miss Flora," he said. "It doesn't matter if you've got your shotgun licence or…" He trailed off, staring at Capstick. Another policeman appeared over Flora's other shoulder. Faced with the full force of the law – and Flora – Capstick dropped the gun.

"You're under arrest for the attempted kidnapping of the Honourable Henry Fairfax…" the police officer began as they marched down. Another two armed officers crept into the crypt as the spiel continued. John was totally surrounded, but just stared blindly in front of him as they cuffed him, and dragged him up into the snow outside. The moment he was out, a paramedic rushed down the steps and began tending to Henry.

Jemima carefully put the jewels that she had removed back into the old red canvas bag, noticing that a few stones had come out of their settings and were sitting in a heap at the bottom. She followed the two paramedics carrying Henry on the stretcher up out of the crypt. Lord Fairfax brought up the rear. She didn't look at John, who stood outside between two more policemen. She didn't know what to say. By now most of the snow between the chapel and the helicopter had been blown away by the its rotors, so it was easier to make their way back. They loaded Henry, still out cold on his stretcher, into the helicopter, followed by Capstick, who was handcuffed into his seat. Jemima stepped in after. Behind her, Rupert and Lord Fairfax, with the pistol in his pocket, had begun riding the horses home. Flora was turning the tractor, about to tow out another police car. As they flew back over the snow-clad land towards the house, Jemima looked down and saw the shape of Henry's beloved horse, fallen over and partially covered in snow and couldn't help but cry. It was a horrible sight.

They landed back in front of the Hall and all disembarked from the police helicopter except for Capstick who was being taken to Bournemouth police station. An air ambulance was waiting near the lake for Henry.

"It's like bloody Bournemouth airport," moaned Lord Fairfax as he came from the direction of the stables with Rupert.

"He'll be absolutely fine," the paramedic reassured Lady Fairfax. "He's been out cold for a bit and he's quite chilled. He'll be in for a night to warm up and rehydrate and make sure there's no concussion. By the sound of it, the hangover's going to be the worst part!" On cue, Henry opened his eyes and groaned. Behind them, Flora chugged slowly up the drive in the tractor, having stopped to liberate another police car stuck in a snowdrift.

Jemima was still clutching the heavy canvas bag full of priceless jewels.

"Is Mama's tiara in there?" asked Flora as she reached her.

"Oh my God – no it's not! I completely forgot about that what with everything else!" The police were just about to leave as Jemima hammered on the window of the car.

"Where's the tiara?" she asked.

"What tiara?" he answered. "I told you. There's never been a tiara."

"Come on, John, it's too late to play games – you're already going to be charged with kidnap and harbouring stolen goods. Royal goods at that."

"I swear – I don't know what you are talking about." He pleaded, looking very worse for wear after his own ordeal down in the crypt. The police car started to move and rolled off down the drive.

"How can it have disappeared then?" asked Flora.

"I think I know," said Jemima. She realised she was shivering. She was still wearing her sodden moonboots and damp salopettes and jacket with her trusty New Look dress underneath. "I'm so cold – can we go inside?" she asked. They trooped into the hall, and Jemima stripped off her damp things in the boot room while no one was looking. She instantly regretted it – casting around she realised there wasn't so much as a spare pair of jeans to put on. Oh God, I can't solve this mystery dressed just in my knickers! she thought desperately. As if summoned by magic, Andrews appeared again, bearing a large whisky, and an enormous quilted silk dressing robe of Lady Fairfax's. Jemima smiled. She could get used to this.

"Wright, could you ask everyone to gather in the drawing room," she requested, and took a sip of whisky – it warmed her from inside out, like spicy honey. She had suddenly worked out who had taken the tiara, and it all made perfect sense from all the bits she had gleaned during the extraordinary day.

It was past midnight by the time they all gathered, and Rupert handed around the remnants of wine from the bottles that had been left in the dining room.

"I think I need a brandy, actually, Rupert darling," Tinkerbell said.

"I still want to know what has happened to Mama's tiara, Jemima, you definitely put it in her room last night?"

"No – I put it in your room, and you said you'd put it in hers. I'd never enter her room!" she protested – her guilty conscience always got out of hand on these occasions. And she looked at Granny Tinkerbell sitting right up by the fire sipping the alcohol from a huge bowl of a glass. "And I think I know who took it."

"Go on, Miss Marple!" Rupert winked flirtatiously.

"If I am wrong, please don't ban me from Fairfax Park," said Jemima. "But I think the person who took the tiara was Granny Tinkerbell."

And as everyone looked over at the old lady, she smiled.

Chapter 14

Fairfax Hall – half past midnight

"Yes, it was me," said Granny Tinkerbell.

"But why?" said the Viscountess, staring stunned at her mother-in-law.

"Jemima dear, you think you've worked it out, don't you? Why don't you tell us?" Granny Tinkerbell sat up expectantly holding the large glass of brandy.

"Right." Jemima took a sip of whisky, crossed the room in her silk robe and sat down on the chair on the other side of the fire holding the letter that she had grabbed from John before he was taken off to the police station.

"We all know that the then Queen Elizabeth, our current Queen's mother," she added for Rupert who looked confused, "hated Wallis Simpson. She was furious that her feckless brother-in-law had lavished so many expensive presents on her, and as the years went by, she wanted more and more to retrieve as many of the Royal jewels he had given his scandalous wife as possible. Remember she later blamed them for her husband's early death. They all wanted to retrieve the set of emeralds that had belonged to Queen Alexandra – yes, they did exist," she added, before anyone could ask. "The Queen Mother thought firstly that they were pieces that should be passed down to her daughter, Elizabeth, as part of the Crown Jewels, but she was also motivated by value. A set of emeralds this size was immensely valuable – and the profligate Wallis had already shown she was wasteful and dissolute with her possessions. The final straw was her trip to England, when she showed up with her trunks and trunks of clothes to a country ravaged by rations and the ruins of war. Rumours had been abounding for some time that Wallis had been selling her jewellery to fund their lifestyle, and I don't think the Queen Mother could bear the thought of the family's emeralds being carved up and carted off to the highest bidder."

Jemima stopped briefly, and turned the confession over in her hand. "A trusted equerry happened to live not far from Windsor Castle and was despatched to engage a local thief with the job of getting back the Royal emeralds. Obviously, this was a job that could only be delegated to the most discrete, but as added protection the thief had to be both a local, and someone with no trace of any previous convictions.

"However, when the thief came to take the emeralds from Wallis's jewellery box, they were gone! The Queen must have been furious – risking so much on the burglary and not even retrieving the emeralds. As part of the deal the thief was allowed to keep what remained of the jewellery – the Royal Family had little use for it, indeed mustn't be caught with it – and it was he who hid it in the crypt at Fairfax Park, as he says in this confession."

Jemima stood up again and walked slowly about the room.

"The Queen Mother knew that Wallis had pulled a fast one on her, and she was powerless to do anything about it. She couldn't admit the emeralds were missing without incriminating the Royal Family, herself, in the heist. However, she was determined to discover the truth. She contacted a young cousin, a ballerina, and a friend of the Windsors, who was close to David, and knew Wallis well enough not to attract suspicion." Jemima now looked directly at Tinkerbell. "Stop me if I get anything wrong."

"Rupert's right, you could very well be Miss Marple!" smiled the old lady. "But do go on – you're on the right track!"

"The day after the theft, you and your husband visited the Windsors and Dudleys at Ednam Lodge. Under pretence of a friendly tea, you wanted to find out if the emeralds had really been stolen – you'd just been told that they were missing from the jewellery box. But while Wallis was happy enough to boast of the size and value of the emeralds, the Windsors kept to the story that they had been stolen and were already working with Lloyd's of London on the claim. You reported this back, and although Scotland Yard, indeed Detective Inspector John

Capstick, spent years quizzing the thief – the emeralds, and the jewels he took, had vanished into thin air."

"Until this morning, that is, when we were talking about the tiara that Flora and I collected from Garrard last night. Because the emeralds weren't quite as gone as you'd thought. I noticed your face when I described it to you."

Jemima paused, wondering where to go next with the story. Granny Tinkerbell helped out, taking a sip of brandy, clearing her throat and continuing.

"No, no they had not. It is true that since the theft we lost track of the emeralds, however—"

"We?" interrupted Flora. "Who's 'We'?"

"Oh, the department of internal affairs, darling," said Granny Tinkerbell calmly. "I mean, one couldn't sit idle. There had been a war on, and afterwards there was the Cold War."

There was a dramatic pause. "Granny," said Flora after a moment. "Were you a spy?"

"Well if that's what you want to call it," Granny Tinkerbell sipped the brandy placidly. "I prefer to think I was just one of a group of friends who kept an eye on another group of friends, in case they fell in with the wrong sort. And being a ballerina, I got to travel and meet people easily."

There was another pause.

"Do you mean the Nazis supporters?" said Rupert.

"Yes," said Granny Tinkerbell serenely. "Bastards the lot of them. Would you like me to continue, Jemima?"

"I've never heard Granny swear before," a wide-eyed

Flora whispered to Rupert.

It was all Jemima could do not to giggle.

"Unbeknown to my cousin Elizabeth Bowes-Lyon, the Queen Mother," she added as explanation, "in the mid-fifties a friend of mine, Jean-Jacques Cartier, let me into a secret; that there was an exceptionally talented jeweller called Jacob Levy working out of a small atelier in Paris. He'd been firm friends with the Cartiers for years; during the war he escaped to England, where he was employed by them in Bond Street. He'd had to escape." She continued, "He was the only one of his family not sent to the gas chambers."

There was a moment's silence.

"In 1946 both he and the Windsors were back in Paris," continued Granny Tinkerbell. "The Duchess of Windsor commissioned him to create a tiara as spectacular as possible, to include ten large emeralds she had with her. He hadn't known the Windsors for long, and he was desperately in need of work, so he took the job and created the most beautiful tiara the century would have ever seen. Had Wallis been granted the Royal recognition, as in the HRH, that she expected, that is. It was after he had made the tiara that the rumours of Wallis's pre-war Nazi leanings reached him. He was of course, still heartbroken about it a decade later. When I met him, he was only too happy to tell me about the emeralds; Wallis had told him that he was to tell no one about the stones – that they had belonged to Queen Alexandra and were priceless – but now he felt betrayed, so he took me into his confidence. He also showed me a photograph of the Woolworth's heiress Jessie Donahue, wearing the tiara – he'd torn up all the ones of Wallis in it."

She took another sip of brandy and continued.

"Well I was stunned, of course. But Wallis had clearly managed to squirrel the tiara away somewhere, so I presumed it would never be seen again. And then," the old lady said in tones of divine retribution, "she had an affair with Jessie Donahue's son Jimmy. That was her downfall. Straight after the theft in 1946, Wallis had given the tiara to Mrs Donahue for safe keeping until she could safely wear it in Europe. Unfortunately, scandalised and horrified by what her former friend had done several years later, Jessie never did return it – and of course Wallis couldn't exactly kick up a fuss. Quite apart from the scandal that sleeping with her friend's much younger son would have caused, after her husband had abdicated for her, she had also claimed on the insurance, and told the Royal Family that their priceless emeralds had been stolen."

"And then Jessie died," picked up Jemima after a moment's pause. "And her jewellery was passed down to her family, where bits of it are still being passed on – including to you, Your Ladyship." She looked across at Viscountess Fairfax who sat rooted to an armchair.

"Well, this sure is interesting." In shock, Jessica had regained her American accent. "I knew that they were special emeralds, that indeed the tiara had been royal, but as many of the women in my family liked to buy up European royal jewels, I didn't think much of it. I thought it was quite splendid!"

"This is what came over with the Astors?" said her husband.

"Well yes. It was only recently passed to me when another relative died – not that long ago in fact. They brought it over in the summer. It was at Garrard where it had been cleaned and repaired a little."

"Oh, so that is why you had it valued – for the insurance?" Flora asked her mother.

"I haven't had it valued for sale." Jessica looked horrified. "It was valued for probate at just under a million dollars. I am afraid I did smuggle it into the country on the Astors' yacht that they brought over from Long Island in the summer," she said. "I'm sorry, William." She turned to her husband. "I should have told you I was bringing home something quite so valuable."

"And stolen," Jemima added bravely. "You must have known of its provenance? That is why you smuggled it in!" she remembered how touchy the Viscountess was when Granny Tinkerbell told the story earlier in the day, maybe it wasn't her worries over Henry.

"I had heard rumours, I admit – but as you said earlier, Tinkerbell, I thought they were just conspiracy theories." She couldn't hide to everyone that she actually knew a lot more about the emeralds than she was letting on.

There was another pause as everyone sipped their drinks and thought about what they'd just realised.

"So, will Mama have to give it back? After all they are stolen emeralds, I suppose?" Flora said looking at both her father and grandmother.

"To be frank – I have no idea. I think we should inform the Royal Family. The emeralds do belong to them," said Lord Fairfax, with a furious and surprised look at his wife of thirty-five years.

"Well actually," Rupert piped up from where he'd been having a quiet brandy in the corner. "They belong to my firm, Lloyd's of London. As do the jewels you have in that bag, Jemima. After all, it seems that we paid out the insurance money."

It was at this moment that Donald, Daphne's boyfriend who'd been sitting in the corner of the room, listening in astonishment, argued. "But that's not right – the Windsors claimed for the emeralds, not the tiara. Surely the tiara itself and the diamonds in it are still the property of Lady Fairfax? They were given to her ancestor by the Duchess, even if only temporarily."

Rupert looked surprised. "Well, yes, I suppose so!"

"Well in that case, surely the emeralds can return to Lloyd's and replacement stones could be found." The director nodded at Lady Fairfax. "After all, I imagine Your Ladyship would want to keep such a beautiful piece in your family, and I'm sure all the biggest jewellery companies would fight over who got to provide the stones for such an historic piece – the Duchess of Windsor's tiara after all. Although," he turned to Jemima with a wink, "with the role of Miss Fox-Pearl in mind, I'm sure I could recommend a very particular name, a jewellery house with a glittering history, whose head of public relations has been so much help to you in all this."

"I'm sure," said Jemima smiling, "Vogel would be only too happy to help."

Epilogue

Boxing Day Morning

By Boxing Day, normality had almost been restored. After the events of Christmas Eve, Henry had been returned from hospital in time for an enormous dinner at 8pm on Christmas Day – which Lady Fairfax claimed was a horrifying break with tradition, but Granny Tinkerbell told Jemima she thought was perfect. After all it was very much in the Fairfax family tradition. They had, of course, dressed up for the occasion, and since Jemima's New Look dress had been ruined, Lady Fairfax pressed upon her a huge gown in emerald raw silk, tightly corseted, as well as the Victorian tiara, which made Jemima look like an eighteenth-century beauty at the French Court. Rupert was in awe.

"This dress is gorgeous," she whispered to Flora during drinks before dinner. "I'm terrified I'm going to spill something down it."

"Don't," advised Flora. "It's one-off Chanel Couture,

Mummy had it made for the Met Ball a few years ago. Karl Lagerfeld himself sewed in the label." Jemima gulped.

On Boxing Day, Jemima and Flora packed their bags. Flora was off skiing in Verbier, and of course Jemima was heading to the Southern Hemisphere that night. She hadn't been able to resist nipping out to the stables before breakfast and taking Bathsheba and Bostik a carrot each. Neither seemed fazed by their night-time dip in the icy stream, in fact Bostik was thoroughly enjoying the renewed attentions of Lord Fairfax, who'd decided that the scrappy little old racehorse was the hero of the yard.

Waiting outside on the steps for the taxi to take her and Flora to their holidays of sun and snow, Jemima realised she didn't really want to leave Fairfax Park, although God knows she was looking forward to the warmth of Cape Town. Even Andrews hadn't been able to save her moonboots. She checked the yellow diamond Vogel engagement ring was safely in her handbag, sitting in a muddle of her own Accessorize jewellery so it wouldn't get remarked upon at airport security, and that Flora had the tiara back in its green leather case. They were being met at the VIP area of Heathrow, where a member of Rupert's fraud investigation office and an equerry of the Royal Family would be taking it back to be investigated. The emeralds would be removed before the tiara was handed on to Vogel to have replacements fitted. Sidney Vogel had called Jemima that morning to congratulate her – he was overjoyed that Vogel's name was now going to be forever linked to the Duchess of Windsor's tiara even though it was caught up in a great deal of scandal! Maybe he was finally figuring out PR, she thought! She suspected it was Danny Vogel who'd tipped off the newspapers – somehow the *Daily Mail* had discovered the story and what with not much else to report on, had organised a telephone interview with Jemima from Cape Town after she landed the following day. Tinkerbell, the Dowager Viscountess, however, was overjoyed to receive a call from someone at the Palace first thing that morning, who praised and thanked her for her long service to the Royal Family.

Jemima couldn't help but feel a bit sorry for John, despite how awful he was. After all, he'd just been trying to prove his grandfather was right – Jemima still didn't think he'd really been trying to take the priceless jewels that had been buried for more than half a century for himself. He would never have been able to sell them on the open market anyway, they were so obviously the Duchess of Windsor's to anyone who knew about jewellery.

The Fairfaxes gathered outside to wave her and Flora off, including Henry – who was being given another lecture by his father about hunting drunk and inviting un-vetted guests home – and Granny Tinkerbell, who kissed Jemima and told her to look after herself, slipped an envelope into her hand. "What's this?" said Jemima.

"For the plane!" the old lady whispered and stepped back.

The girls leant back in the seats as the taxi swept out of the gates and on to a very slushy lane.

"Good Christmas, girls?" the driver said, looking at

them in the rear-view mirror.

They looked at each other and giggled.

"Priceless!" said Jemima smiling as a bunch of text messages beeped on her phone now that they were finally in signal. 'You'll be in trouble for checking out the competition. Garrard…?', it was from Danny and the answer to whoever was stalking them on Bond Street. She sighed with relief, then cringed – there was definitely a similarity between John Capstick and Danny Vogel.

She looked down at the thick creamy envelope, stamped with Fairfax Hall on the rear, which Granny Tinkerbell had given her. It was stuffed full of papers – letters, press cuttings about a heist, diagrams and an invitation to the wedding of Prince Rainier of Monaco and Grace Kelly in 1956.

She turned the envelope back over. There on the front, in Granny Tinkerbell's elegant slanted writing, was written:

'A future mystery – should life take you to Monaco?'

The End

Notes

I have always been quite fascinated by the jewels of the Duchess of Windsor, and was thrilled when my old boss Laurence Graff told me that he had bought the emerald engagement ring for his wife. He also showed me the catalogue of the sale of her exquisite jewellery which took place at Sotheby's in Geneva in 1987. And then I read in a book by Suzy Menkes, *The Crown Jewels*, that there had been a theft of her jewels in 1946 from the Earl of Dudley's country house, Ednam Lodge. It was thought that emeralds which had belonged to Queen Alexandra, and were given to her by her sister Maria Feodorovna – mother of the last Tsar of Russia, had been stolen along with the rest of the jewels. The Duke of Windsor had received them from her when he was the Prince of Wales and given them to the then Wallis Simpson. The story fascinated me. I have loosely based my story on this historic theft. There was indeed an article in the *Daily Telegraph*, December 2003, about a Leslie Holmes and Detective Inspector John Capstick. Capstick had been on the case of the missing jewels and had never given up the belief that Holmes had done it – although he never confessed. The jewels have never been found, nor anyone charged. I set the mystery in Dorset which is where I grew up. Fairfax Hall, and the enormous Fairfax Park, is set in my favourite part of the county – on the coast somewhere near West Bexington.

Acknowledgments

I would firstly like to thank Wiggy Bamforth. There is no way this story would be what it is now, if wasn't for Wiggy's attention to detail in editing and suggesting/ rewriting bits to make them not only far funnier – but far more Jemima Fox. I hope that she is forever my partner in (writing) crime! Secondly my husband Ben for taking such good care of our baby Arthur, to whom this is dedicated, when I have been up all hours writing, and unable to get up yet again to sooth a teething baby in the middle of the night! And for being an endlessly patient husband, listening to my dreams of being a successful author whilst being unable to write!

I'd like to thank Adam Norton for the most beautiful tiara design on the cover, such a powerful inspiration to keep writing. And Luisa Berta for redesigning the cover.

I really hope that you enjoy this novella as much as I enjoyed writing it, and reissuing it with my baby girl beside me!

Jemima Fox will be back in her fourth mystery, The Paris Connection, before too long.

Happy Christmas!
Josie
24th November 2019

About the Author

Josie Goodbody worked in PR and Marketing in London for several of the world's top fine jewellery houses, as well as writing about jewellery for magazines. After a year living in Monaco, followed by three in Argentina and Uruguay, Josie now lives on the Dorset/ Wiltshire borders with her husband, son and daughter, and her little dog Milo.

This is her second book; her third in the Jemima Fox series, The Monte Carlo Connection came out in the Summer 2019. The Diamond Connection is the first book of the series. All the books are available on Amazon and distributors worldwide.

Lightning Source UK Ltd.
Milton Keynes UK
UKHW042338051219
354840UK00003B/102/P

9 781916 146754